COMBUST

(Electric Series #4)

E. L. TODD

Fallen Publishing

Combust

Editing Services provided by Final-Edits.com

Chapter One

Volt

A week came and went.

My hand was glued to my phone as I waited for a text message or a phone call. I took my phone everywhere I went. It was even on the counter while I took a shower just in case I needed to grab it. When I slept, I placed it on my chest so I would instantly know if it rang.

But Taylor never called.

I was supposed to be patient and give her space. I was supposed to be understanding and calm.

But I was beginning to realize how incapable I was of doing such things.

I hated my apartment with every fiber of my being. It still smelled like her, contained her old whispers as they echoed in the corners. A pair of her socks was still in my top drawer—along with a thong. Everything she left behind just tortured me.

Because she wasn't there.

Once upon a time, I loved being alone. I loved having my own space and my own silence. Isolation was my comfort. But now, the silence was terrifying. The absence of her voice and her laughter was crippling.

I couldn't take it anymore.

That's when my hand started to shake, reaching for the phone with restless fingers. I wanted to call her just to hear her voice. I wanted to beg her to come back to me. Being desperate wasn't in my nature, but with her, I folded all my cards.

Then strength came back to me, and I put the phone down.

Instead, I just stared at it.

***

How long did I have to wait?

I couldn't hold my silence any longer.

A week was long enough.

She should be ready to talk by now.

Right?

Even though I knew I should stay away, I couldn't do it anymore. Seven full days was long enough, and I couldn't wait another minute. No, I couldn't even wait another second.

I arrived at her doorstep and knocked. My hands dug into the pockets of my jeans, and I felt my shoulders sag. Now that my happiness was gone, I wasn't sure how to go on without it. How would I go back to my bed without her beside me? How would I get up in the morning when I had no motivation to do anything?

She opened the door, her movements slow and her eyes hesitant. She didn't hate the fact I was there but she wasn't excited to see me either. She kept one hand on the door like she suspected this conversation would be quick.

That wasn't a good sign.

"Hey."

Now that I was standing on her doorstep, I didn't know how to proceed. My heart wanted to dump all my emotional turmoil on her shoulders, but I knew that wouldn't get me anywhere. Like a manipulative diplomat, I had to do this carefully. "How are you?"

"I'm okay. You?"

Horrible. Terrible. I can't sleep. Can't eat. "Good."

She leaned against the door and turned her gaze to the ground, unsure what else to do.

I kept my hands in my pockets, feeling the tension rise further. If our conversation was this strained, then she clearly wasn't ready to talk. I should just walk away and try a different time. But now that I could see her, I didn't want to leave. I missed her. Staring at her beautiful face gave me some form of peace. Her lips looked kissable like always, and it took all my strength not to grab her face and lay a hard kiss on her pretty little mouth. "How's work?"

"It's okay," she said. "The kids are anxious for winter break so they're monsters right now."

"Nothing you can't handle."

She didn't smile or acknowledge the compliment.

She had a steel wall erected around her, and my catapults of conversation bounced back at me. "I just wanted to stop by and check on you. See if you were doing okay."

"I'm fine," she said. "It's been rough, but I'll make it through."

What kind of response was that? What did she mean when she said she would make it through? "Can I come in?"

"Uh..." She eyed her apartment behind her, unsure how to answer.

I didn't wait for one. I walked inside and didn't look back.

She shut the door behind me before she came to my side. "Would you like a drink?"

"I'm okay." The only thing I wanted to drink was her. What I really needed was an embrace. I wanted to wrap my arms around her and cherish the smell of her hair. I wanted my arms to hang off her feminine hips. I wanted to feel her heart beat against my chest, faint through our clothing. That's what I needed.

"Okay." She crossed her arms over her chest, keeping two feet between us.

She was purposely keeping me at a distance, refusing to let me get too close to her, physically and metaphorically.

"What have you been up to?" I was reaching for anything. Conversations used to flow so feely with her. Now they hung in the air, stagnant and intolerable.

"Just been staying at home. I haven't really wanted to go out."

Me too.

"What about you?"

"Pretty much the same." Except wanting to die every second of the day.

"Hold on a sec. I'll be right back." She entered the hallway and then her bedroom.

Maybe I should have followed her and pinned her to the mattress. I could have forced her to be mine, gotten her to fall for me like she had so many times. We could get swept away in the mutual desire and everything else would fade away.

But that would make me an asshole.

Taylor returned a moment later with a box in her hands. Inside were some of my old t-shirts and sweatpants, as well as my toothbrush and other toiletries. "I've been meaning to give this to you."

I stared at it blankly, unable to process exactly what it meant. It was too painful, too scarring. Taking a single breath was impossible because it hurt so much. My hand remained in my pockets as I stared at the box that contained my belongings. My eyes slowly turned to her, and I couldn't mask the pain.

She couldn't handle looking at me, so she looked away.

"Why are you doing this to me?" I couldn't stop my voice from escaping as a threat. I couldn't keep my cool anymore. She was torturing me.

"Volt...I think it's time we move on."

Move on? "No. We aren't moving on. I thought you just needed some space. Then you do this to me..."

"I'm not trying to hurt you."

I yanked the box out of her hand and tossed it on the ground. "I'm not taking it so don't bother."

Her hands still hung in the air from where they held the box. She slowly lowered them.

"I know we had a bad fight, and I made an ass out of myself, but breaking up isn't the solution. We'll get through it. Take all the time you need, but don't throw my stuff at me."

"Volt, we already broke up. This isn't news."

"No. We. Didn't." If she thought I was letting her get away, she was stupid. If she tried to wiggle out of my grasp, I would just hold on tighter. We loved each other too damn much to go our separate ways.

Way too fucking much.

She closed her eyes, trying to keep herself grounded. "This isn't easy for me either."

"It looked pretty easy when you threw my shit at me."

When she opened her eyes, she didn't look at me. She looked past me, like eye contact was too intimate.

"I'll apologize as many times as it takes. I'll do whatever you want to make this work. I'm not giving up on us."

"Volt, you don't get it."

"Clearly."

Her gaze turned to me. "It's not gonna work. I love you. You know I do. But...I can't repeat myself again."

"Well, you're going to have to. Because I don't get it."

She crossed her arms over her chest, closing off from me again.

"I know I fucked up. I'm not making excuses for myself. But I promise you I won't act that way again. I'll never treat you that way again. I'm sorry from the bottom of my goddamn heart. Don't take away something that's good for both of us. Remember what we had and focus on that, not that one terrible week."

She was still as a statue and just as quiet. "Everything is different now, Volt. I don't look at you the same way I used to."

Every word was breaking my heart. It was already snapped in two and would never repair itself, not at this rate.

"Yes, you do."

"No, I don't."

"You still love me. That's all that matters."

"But I don't trust you. And you clearly don't trust me."

"Not true. I just…flipped out one time. Don't hold that against me when I'm nothing but perfect for you the rest of the time."

"I'm not saying you weren't good to me. Because you were. What we had…was beautiful. But that was at the beginning of the relationship when it's all sex and talking. The second we hit a bump in the road, you went off the deep end. There are going to be a lot of bumps in the road, and I can't be with a man with your kind of temper. I can't be with a man who speaks to me that way. I can't walk on egg shells whenever we disagree."

I closed my eyes as the self-loathing enveloped me. My rampage ruined everything, and I couldn't blame her for holding it against me. I was out of my mind, and nothing I said would convince her that was just a fluke. When I'd been wronged in the past, I never behaved that way. It was just a one-time thing. But she would never believe me.

"I love you. I do. But…I'm sorry."

I never thought I would be happy again, and then Taylor walked into my life. She fixed everything, made me whole. And just as quickly, she was taken away from me, leaving me desolated in the middle of the hottest desert.

She took a step back, her arms still across her chest. "I think you should go."

There was nothing left for me there. I said what I needed to say, and I heard all the things I wasn't ready to listen to. The fight died inside me, sitting in the back of my throat.

"I'm not trying to hurt you. I swear."

"Well, you are." I turned my back on her, unable to look her in the eye. My shoulders were stiff with pain and my heart stung in rejection. Everything hurt, from the tip of my toes to the end of my nose.

Taylor didn't say another word as she watched me walk out of the apartment. She didn't try to hand over the box of my belongings. She let me go in silence.

Was this just as painful for her as it was for me?

Did she want to die just the way I did?

Or was I the only one who felt this crippling pain?

***

Clay studied me from across the table, his fingers wrapped around a mechanical pencil. "You alright, man?"

"I'm fine." I hadn't slept in a week, I wasn't eating, and I couldn't concentrate on a single thought for more than a minute—unless I was thinking about Taylor. She ruined me, crippled me beyond repair.

"You don't seem fine..."

"I'm just hung over." That should get him to back off.

"No, you aren't," he said. "I'm seventeen, not stupid."

"Just get off my back, alright?" I leaned back in the chair and crossed my arms over my chest. "Get to work. Your exam is right around the corner. Don't waste any more time."

"I'm worried about you." He shut the book, giving me a vulnerable look that didn't appear very often. "What happened?"

"It's just..." I realized I told Clay things I never told anyone else. He'd become my confidant, my friend. "Taylor left me."

He stared at me with the same expression, unsure what that phrase meant. "Left you?"

"She broke up with me," I explained. "I did something really stupid, and I paid the price for it."

"I'm sorry, Volt. I know she made you happy."

"Yeah...she did." And I would never be that happy again.

Clay dug into his pocket until he pulled out a sucker. It was the kind that had caramel in the middle and it was covered by sticky sour apple sugar. "You like candy?"

It was all he had, and he was choosing to give it to me. The gesture wasn't lost on me, and I wouldn't offend him. "Thanks. Just what I need." I snatched it from his hand and pulled the wrapper off. "Who needs good teeth?"

Chapter Two

Taylor

I was miserable.

It was exactly what I expected, but it hurt more than I anticipated. Asking Volt to leave and give up on us was hard—more difficult than I let on. When everything was said and done, I still loved him.

I would always love him.

But if that kind of explosion happened so early in our relationship, did we really stand a chance? He called me a whore and pushed me around like a rag doll. He revealed his true colors, his uncontrollable temper.

Could I really be involved with someone like that?

I thought Volt was my Prince Charming. I thought I finished kissing my share of frogs and finally found my happily ever after.

But I was wrong.

I went to work every day like I usually did, going through the motions but not truly being there. Mr. Davidson came by like he usually did, but he returned to being a colleague and a friend. Natalie usually stopped by and asked more questions about Volt.

Just when I stopped thinking about him.

When I was home, I sat on the couch and watched TV. I neglected my schoolwork because I didn't care anymore. I didn't care about anything at the moment—except Volt.

I wasn't sure what would happen to the gang, but since Volt was friends with everyone before I came into the picture, I thought it was best if I took a step back. I still saw Natalie every day at work, so it was okay. It wasn't like I wouldn't ever see her again.

I flipped through the channels because there was nothing on TV. Well, there was nothing on because I'd already watched everything. I'd seen every western, every classic, and every action movie they played on daytime television. I watched re-runs of Friends and didn't laugh once.

That's when there was a knock on the door.

My heart jolted in hope, wanting Volt to be standing on the other side. I broke up with him, but I still wanted him. He was still in my dreams every night. When I woke up in the morning, I felt his side of the bed, expecting him to be there.

And then I remembered he was gone.

I checked the peephole and was disappointed to see Derek had paid me a visit. With the blanket still draped over my arms, I opened the door. "Hi."

Derek looked me up and down, seeing my old pajamas with a spaghetti stain on the t-shirt and the dirty blanket I continued to hide under. "I just talked to Volt."

"Yes, everything you've heard is true." I walked back to the couch and plopped down on the cushion. I immediately pulled my knees to my chest and returned my attention to the TV.

Derek sat beside me, his eyes glued to the side of my face. "He's miserable, in case you didn't know."

I did know.

"And you look even more miserable. So, let's just cut the shit and go to his place."

"Cut the shit?" I asked coldly.

"You guys took forever to get together. And I mean, forever. So just work out your differences and understand what's important here. He loves you, and you love him."

"I do love him. And I know he loves me." I kept my eyes glued to the screen.

"Then make it work. Come on, I hate seeing my best friends like this. I've never seen him so low."

And I've never been so low. "Did he tell you what happened?"

He shifted his weight uncomfortably, giving me an answer without actually saying anything. "Yeah...he did."

Enough said.

"I admit that was pretty off-the-wall. And harsh. But I wouldn't have believed any of that happened unless I heard it from his lips—because that's not Volt. I've never seen him snap at anyone before. I'm not trying to belittle what happened to you, but I can honestly say he'll never do that again. Give the guy another chance."

"I can get over all of those things. Everyone makes mistakes. I'm not an exception to that." I turned my face to his, seeing the hope in his eyes. "And it's not really about his behavior. I can forgive the names he called me, the way he grabbed me, and putting me through hell for a week. Because I love him. Of course I can forgive him."

"Then go talk to him," he whispered. "Please."

I wasn't finished. "But I can't forgive why it happened. He jumped to conclusions instead of talking to me about what he saw. If he trusted me like he claimed, he would have asked me about it. Maybe he would have yelled and screamed at me, but he still should have confronted me about it—face-to-face. Instead, he dumped me without telling me what was going on. If I hadn't figured it out, what would have happened? I never would have known why our relationship fell apart. People in real relationships don't act that way. His behavior just tells me he doesn't trust me—and he never trusted me."

"I can see why you feel that way...but I don't agree."

"Not to be rude, but I don't care what you believe."

He flinched at the insult. "Look, I don't exactly know what happened to Volt in the past. He had this girlfriend and they were pretty serious. One day, they just broke up. He never explained why, and he acted like nothing ever happened. And that's when he changed. He became this playboy, sex-a-holic type of guy. I think that has something to do with it. Cut him some slack."

"If that were true, he would have told me."

"I've been his best friend for a long ass time, and he's never even told me about it. Whatever happened really killed him inside. Maybe he'll never tell anyone what happened."

"But if that was relevant to our break up, he would say something. If it were vital to us staying together, he would tell me. Therefore, I don't think it's related." I wish that were the case just so I had an excuse to forgive him.

Derek sighed in defeat.

"Derek, I don't want it to be like this—truly."

He bowed his head. "I know."

"And if it were any other guy, you would tell me to run for the hills."

He didn't agree with me but he didn't need to.

"So I have to walk away."

"I know. I get it. It's just...he was so happy."

"I know." My eyes slowly watered just thinking about it. I missed the way he used to kiss me. I missed the way he used to make love to me. I missed the way he used to look at me. Knowing I would never feel any of those things again broke my heart. "I was happy too."

***

"I think you're being annoying as fuck." Natalie stood next to me at the bar, wearing a skintight dress with a gold bracelet dangling from her wrist. "Volt is a huge catch. Any girl in this bar would kill to be with him. Don't throw him away."

I already told her the story, but it didn't seem to matter to her. "I don't want to talk about this anymore."

"Because you know I'm right."

"No. Because everyone needs to let this go."

"Are you telling me you actually think you're going to find another guy you'll love as much as Volt? Do you actually think you'll find someone else who makes you just as happy? I'm telling you right now, guys as handsome, rich, and sweet as Volt don't come around very often."

"So I should let him treat me however he wants?" I snapped.

"No, I just—"

"Nat, you're the one who left a great guy to be with Jared, even though Jared pulled you on a string for three years. I don't judge you for the choices you make so don't judge mine."

Natalie finally shut her mouth after I laid that one on her. But I could tell it cut deep into her skin and charred her core. She set her glass down and turned away. "I need to powder my nose..." She walked off and headed to the bathroom, her shoulders a little heavier than before.

I growled to myself and set my glass down. Why did I have to snap at her like that? In my heart, I knew she was trying to help me. I just hated it when people told me what to do.

"You look like you need a refill." A handsome man came out of nowhere and placed a drink beside me. "Cosmo, right?"

I never took drinks from strangers. He seemed like a nice guy who wouldn't drug anyone, and I highly doubted the drink was spiked, so I chose to be nice to him. "You guessed right."

"I'm glad your friend walked away. Now I get my airtime."

"I hope you shine."

"I'm Ashton. I just moved here not too long ago."

"You'll love the city—after you get used to it. Where did you move from?"

"Iowa."

"Oh, wow. This is a really big change then."

"Yeah, no barns." He chuckled.

I chuckled too.

"I'm sorry, but I didn't catch your name."

"Taylor."

"Very pretty." He drank the beer he was holding in his hand. "Well, Taylor, I think it's safe to say we have pretty good chemistry. Maybe we should have dinner together sometime. You can pick the place."

There was no way in hell I was dating someone, not when Volt and I just broke up. Honestly, I couldn't see myself ever dating again. My entire body had shut down, and I couldn't feel even a hint of arousal for anyone but him. "I'm very flattered but—" I felt a shadow pass overhead, like a heavy raincloud blocking out the sun. It hovered right on top of me, making me anticipate the thunder as well as the lightning. Threat filled the air, making every muscle in my body tense with fear.

I looked up to see Volt standing there, looking absolutely frightening. His face was expressionless but his eyes gave away his warning. He wanted to snap the guy's neck for breathing the same air I did. He wanted to strangle him for getting too close. And he wanted to give me an earful about this kind of betrayal.

He turned to Ashton, squaring his shoulders and intimidating him with a simple look. "Go."

Ashton didn't need to be told twice. He turned away and tried to get the hell out of there.

"Wait." Volt grabbed the cosmo and shoved it into the guy's chest. "Take your piss with you."

Ashton grabbed it with a shaky hand and didn't complain about the front of his shirt getting soaked. Then he hauled ass.

Volt took his place in front of me, looking like a king about to execute one of his citizens.

"What the hell was that?" I snapped. "He was a nice guy, and you didn't need to behave like that."

He stared me down, the vein in his neck throbbing. "We just broke up, and you're already picking up guys in bars? That's how much I meant to you? What the fuck, Taylor?"

"I'm not picking up guys. I was just—"

"Wearing a skin tight dress and flirting with some guy after he bought you a drink. I think it's pretty goddamn clear."

"Volt—"

"I'm depressed out of my mind while you're out having a good time. Maybe we are broken up, but this is just wrong. I can't believe how little I mean to you."

"I wasn't going to go out with him."

"Yeah, sure," he said sarcastically.

My temper came out in full force. "Like you haven't screwed a dozen women by now."

His eyes narrowed. "You really think I would do that?"

"I don't know. You tell me." I wanted to know he hadn't been with anyone but me. I wanted to know I was still the only one. Maybe if that were true, we could work on our relationship. Maybe we could take baby steps. But if he said otherwise, I would die inside.

"You know what? This break up is the best thing that ever happened to me." He grabbed my drink and completely downed it in a single gulp. "I give my heart to someone and she stomps all over it. I knew this would happen. I convinced myself you were different but you aren't. You're just like all the others." He slammed the glass on the counter so hard it shattered. He didn't blink an eye as the glass scattered everywhere. "Now excuse me, I have somewhere to be." He walked off and disappeared in the back of the room.

I stayed in my spot and watched the glass reflect the overhead lights. Drops of the cocktail sprinkled across the counter. When I was face-to-face with him, I was able to keep my composure. But the second he was gone, I felt my sobs start deep in my chest. I didn't want to cry because I hated the feeling. But I knew it was coming.

And I couldn't stop it.

***

Two weeks went by and I didn't hear anything from Volt.

He probably screwed a dozen more women by now.

I blocked out the thought because it would cripple me all over again, just like last time.

In an effort to move forward, I tried to never think about him. I put the box of his stuff deep in the back of my closet so I wouldn't see it again. I completely changed my bedding so nothing would remind me of him. I gave the apartment a deep clean so not even his essence would remain behind.

But I couldn't stop the dreams.

He always came to me when I was asleep. He wasn't aggressive and rude like he was in real life. He was tender and loving, just the way he used to be. Those dreams were the worst because I always woke up crying, missing those days more than I missed home.

The two weeks passed at a snail's pace. Somehow, being miserable made time go by even slower. Every second felt like a minute, and every minute felt like an hour. I'd never felt heart beak like this.

It was so much worse because he was my best friend.

And now he was gone.

Sara was my other best friend, but I didn't tell her everything like I told him. We used to spend every free moment together, playing video games or just lying on the couch.

And now it was over.

Maybe I shouldn't have gotten involved with him at all. Now I lost my boyfriend and my best friend. But could I regret something that gave me so much joy? Our time together was short—but it was beautiful.

Natalie and Sara were there for me, taking me out to do things a few times a week. But they never asked me about Volt. They didn't mention his name. Sometimes I wanted Natalie to bring him up just so I would know how he was doing. But hearing about him would just make it worse.

As time went on, my longing intensified. I missed him more and more, and I found myself crying in between classes because I suddenly felt the hole in my chest. He was gone from my life—forever. I couldn't handle the loss. I couldn't handle the fact he was gone.

Everything was too much.

Christmas was just around the corner, and I would have two weeks off from school. I wanted to go home and see my family, but I just couldn't afford it. I didn't want to spend the holiday alone, but my checking account simply couldn't support a cross-country trip. And now I was seriously thinking about quitting my job.

I couldn't work at Bristol Academy anymore.

Volt's father would eventually find out what happened between Volt and I, and working with him would just be awkward. Plus, I didn't want to see anything that reminded me of Volt.

It was too painful.

So I had to leave.

Chapter Three

Volt

My anger lasted for a full week.

I went on a crazy tantrum, insulting everyone who came too close to me. Seeing Taylor mingling with a guy at a bar pissed me the fuck off. I was licking my wounds and trying to get through another day, and she was out flirting with her next guy.

Fuck her.

I tried to pick up a few women to bring back to my place. I wanted to fuck them so hard that my headboard broke. I wanted to hurt Taylor the way she hurt me.

But I couldn't do it.

After talking with them for a few moments, I chickened out. The idea of touching someone besides Taylor made me sick. There was no way I could even get hard. And I would be doing it for the wrong reasons. I would get no enjoyment out of it, only pain.

Had she slept with anyone?

Was she out and about, casually dating and sleeping around?

The idea of anyone touching her made me want to hurl. She was my girl. Even if we weren't together anymore, she was still mine. If she slept with someone else, it would feel like a betrayal. If she fell in love with someone else, it would kill me.

It would kill me again.

Christmas was coming, and I was dreading the holidays. My parents kept asking if Taylor was coming for Christmas day, and I didn't have the heart to tell them we broke up.

It was too hard to say it out loud.

Everyone was getting excited for the season, and I couldn't care in the least. The only thing that made me happy was gone. She walked out on me and broke my heart at least five times in a row.

I wish I'd never fallen in love with her.

I was moping around at home when Derek came by. He was spending a lot more time with me, trying to get my mind off Taylor. He didn't bring her up because it always made things worse when he did. I didn't want to talk about her or think about her.

I wish I could forget about her.

He brought over a case of beer and handed me one. "IPA?"

"Sure." As long as it had alcohol in it, I didn't care.

He sat beside me and we watched the game in comfortable silence.

I hated my apartment. It still reeked of Taylor. I made love to her right on this couch. She sat on my lap and bounced on my dick. I thrust into her from underneath, and we both got washed away in the mutual pleasure.

I didn't want to be single again. I just wanted to be with her, to have that amazing relationship again. How could I lose something so amazing? How could she walk away from me so easily? How could she start dating again?

Derek cleared his throat once a commercial came on. "Okay, don't get mad at me."

He was going to mention Taylor. And I really didn't want to hear about it. "How about we just skip it and sit in silence?"

Derek set his beer on the coffee table and rubbed his chin. "You're going to hate me for a little bit but hear me out."

"I'd rather not."

"I really think you should tell her about what happened with Sara."

I immediately gritted my teeth when he mentioned that name. I was already pissed off, but now I was livid. I hated thinking about that skank. She broke my heart and screwed me over. Even now, I hadn't recovered from it.

"I still don't know what happened, but I know whatever went down is affecting your relationship with Taylor."

"What relationship? We don't have a relationship."

Derek ignored the question. "You've never been the same since you broke up with Sara. You went on a sex rampage and didn't stop until Taylor came into your life. I think you flipped out like that because of something Sara did. Am I right?"

I refused to answer.

"Tell Taylor that. I really think it will make a difference."

"It won't make any difference at all."

"How will you know unless you try?"

"She's already dating other guys."

"No, she's not," he argued. "Nat just told me Taylor only leaves the house when Nat drags her out."

I wanted that to be true—so much.

"She's not seeing anyone, man. Stop pushing her away. If you wait too long, it really will be too late."

I looked out the window just to avoid his stare.

"Volt, come on."

"Why do you care so much?" I snapped.

"Because you're my friend. And I remember how happy you were. Don't you want to be happy again?"

I shrugged.

"Yes, you do. Just talk to her. What harm could it do?"

"It could kill me all over again."

"Volt—"

"I said no."

"Nat told me she's looking for a new job, somewhere outside the city. She's actually looking for jobs in Washington. So, if she gets hired somewhere, she's going to leave forever. And you'll miss your chance."

"I already did miss my chance."

He sighed in frustration. "She's putting in her two weeks right after Christmas. And I doubt she'll stick around after that."

I had no idea what she was doing for Christmas, probably seeing her folks in Washington. They would ask about me, and she would say we're done. Maybe she'd bring some other guy with her.

31

Derek stared at me like he expected me to say something.

"What?"

"That's it? You're just giving up?"

"She gave up on us a long time ago."

"And you're going to let her? I'm giving you one last chance to make this right. Do it and if it doesn't work, you can move on. She'll be living on the other side of the country. But if you do nothing...you'll regret it."

The game came back on so I stared at the screen, purposely trying to avoid him.

Derek kept looking at me, silently pressuring me.

I was pissed off at Taylor. Livid, actually. But I couldn't deny how heartbroken I was. Even if she slept with someone else, I'd probably take her back anyway. That's how much I missed her. "It'll have to wait until after New Year's. She'll be in Washington until then."

"She's staying home," Derek said. "Can't afford the flight."

I finally met his gaze. "She's spending Christmas alone?"

"We invited her over, but she didn't want to. Looks like she wants to be alone."

I was a coldhearted person, but even I didn't like being alone on Christmas.

"So, you'll talk to her?" he asked.

When he laid out everything that way, I felt obligated to do something. I felt motivated to give it one more try and hope for the best. If it didn't work out, I could move on because I knew I did everything possible to fix all my mistakes.

"Volt?" he pressed.

"Fine," I whispered. "I'll talk to her."

***

I waited outside her apartment for nearly thirty minutes before I found the courage to knock. My knuckles tapped against the wood and echoed in the hallway. It was unusually silent since everyone left the city to spend the holiday with their families. Christmas Eve was the next day, and the snow was heavy.

Not a single sound echoed from inside her apartment. Her footsteps were silent and the place seemed abandoned. The crack under the door didn't show any light coming from within.

Maybe she managed to scrounge up the money to book a flight.

I'd have to wait until after the holidays to have this dreadful conversation.

To my surprise, the door opened.

Taylor stood there in sweatpants and a t-shirt. The shirt was a little lopsided, like she quickly threw it on when she heard the doorbell ring. She stared at me with surprise, just as shocked to see me across her threshold as I was to see that she actually answered the door. "Hi..."

"Hey." Her hair was pulled back in a high ponytail and her face was free of makeup. She clearly wasn't expecting company. She was expecting to be alone. To me, she looked more beautiful than if she got dressed up. Because this was really her. This was exactly how she looked when she woke up in the morning. This was exactly how she looked when we laid on the couch together. That vulnerability, that truthfulness, was something I truly adored.

I missed it.

The surprise slowly left her face as she looked at me, understanding I was really there.

Without asking first, I walked inside and shut the door behind me. I didn't want to have this conversation in the doorway.

She backed up, giving me room to stand in her small entryway.

That's when I noticed the shirt underneath her kitchen table. It was gray and too many sizes too big. It was an odd place to put her clothes since she was usually neat all the time.

Then I realized it was my shirt.

She was wearing it when I came to the door. When she realized it was me, she quickly changed and tried to hide it so I wouldn't notice.

But I did notice.

And that gave me some hope.

"I'm sorry to bother you, but I was hoping we could talk...if you have time." The last time I saw her, I insulted her before I stormed off. I was too angry to see reason. But now, I was unusually calm, wanting to make sure I didn't scare her away.

"Uh, sure." She crossed her arms over her chest, protecting her heart from my grasp.

"I think I know how this conversation is going to end. I want you to know that I'm prepared to walk out that door and never bother you again. I'm prepared to let you go—for good. But I want to say this first."

Her eyes never left my face. "Okay."

"I've been miserable without you. Even when I'm mad, I'm miserable. Being angry is an easier emotion for me to handle than sadness, and it allows me to push you away...but only for so long. Then I miss you even more than I did before."

Her eyes coated with moisture, but it was only a thin layer. I wasn't even sure if I really saw it.

"Derek told me you're quitting your job and leaving...probably to get away from me. It makes sense. If we keep seeing each other, neither one of us are going to move on. I know I can't."

She didn't nod but I knew she agreed with me.

"This isn't easy for me to say... I've never told anyone this before. I'm not even sure why it haunts me so much. Maybe because I was so genuine and honest...and then I was backstabbed. I don't know. But maybe it'll mean something to you. Maybe it'll piece everything together."

She came closer to me so she could listen to every word.

"I was in a relationship a few years ago. She was a nice girl. Beautiful, smart, and funny. We met at a bar downtown, and we just clicked. At that time, I wasn't the kind of guy who slept around. I usually had short-term relationships with women before they died out. But I'd always been looking for the right person to spend my life with. When I met her, I thought I found the right woman. We were together for about a year and everything was great. She met my parents, and they loved her. And I loved her..." Thinking about this was bringing back painful memories. I didn't want to think about it anymore, but I had to keep moving forward. Taylor needed to know. Perhaps everything would make sense. "I decided to ask her to marry me. I didn't need to be with her any longer to know she was the one. I bought the ring, told my parents, and then called up the guys. Everyone was really excited."

Taylor didn't blink as she stared at me, hanging on to every word. Her arms tightened over her chest like she didn't want to hear what came next.

"I told the guys to meet me at a bar I was near. I walked inside to get a table while I waited for them and that's when..." I still remembered that moment with detailed clarity. I remember the song that came over the speakers, the guys at the nearby table laughing at their friend when he fell out of his chair. I remembered the baseball game on the TV in the corner. The Yankees were playing the Dodgers, and they were up by four. I wore a gray t-shirt with dark blue jeans. The ring sat heavy in my pocket, in the black box it came in. "Her arms were wrapped around his neck and they were kissing. And not just kissing, but kissing hard. They made out for nearly a minute before I stopped staring. The guy she was with was her ex. They broke up shortly before she and I got together. I watched them together and felt like an idiot. I just spent ten thousand dollars on a woman who didn't give a damn about me."

Taylor's eyes watered and she didn't keep the emotions back. They came pouring out, cascading down her cheeks. Her chest heaved from her uneven breaths. "What did you do?"

"I wanted to walk over there and tell her off. I wanted to punch the guy in the face. I wanted to rip that bar apart. But then I realized none of it mattered. If she was hooking up with her ex, then she didn't care about me. What would yelling at her accomplish? Why should I let her know how much she hurt me? It seemed pointless at the time. So I walked out."

"And that's it?" she whispered.

"I met her the next day and told her we were over. She kept asking why, and I told her I didn't really have a reason, I just didn't want her anymore. She cried and begged me to stay. I had to stop myself from laughing. I realized not telling her the truth was a much worse punishment than being honest with her. She was never honest with me, so I didn't owe her anything."

Taylor still breathed hard, feeling all the pain running through my body. She felt exactly what I felt, carrying the burden with me.

"I tell you this because...when I saw you with that guy in your classroom, everything came rushing back. I felt everything I felt that night but a million times worse. Somehow, I love you more than I ever loved her and seeing you betray me just...made me snap. I hadn't been in a relationship in a long time just because I didn't trust anyone. Then I trusted you and it bit me in the ass. I know it's not an excuse. I know it doesn't justify what I did. But I hope it explains everything a little better. I hope it makes you understand that you weren't the problem. The issue was with me. It had nothing to do with not trusting you." I bowed my head when I finished speaking. I said everything I needed to say, and I just hoped it was enough. That was my most painful secret, and I didn't tell anyone about it because I didn't want their sympathy. And I didn't want to be judged for being so goddamn blind. Who knew how long they were fooling around until I caught them? I immediately got a test done to make sure I didn't have an STD. Thankfully, I didn't.

"Volt, I'm so sorry…" She moved into my chest and pressed her cheek against me. Her arms wrapped around me and held me tightly. She hadn't been this close to me in weeks, and it immediately felt nice.

I wasn't offended by her pity, and I took advantage of the situation. My arms wrapped around her petite frame, and I held her tightly, feeling the pain course through my body at being reunited with her. I thought the connection would feel good, but it actually felt painful. It was like liquid nitrogen. It was so cold it was actually hot.

"She's an idiot, Volt. I'm sorry you had to go through that."

It didn't bother me anymore now that Taylor was in my arms. I wanted to take her in the bedroom and hold her all night long. I wanted to cherish this feeling forever and never let it slip away. If she slept with another guy, I'd be devastated, but I would let it go—because she was worth it.

She peered up at me, her eyes still full of tears. "I would never do that to you."

"I know." I always knew that even if I didn't show it. "I'm sorry I let my insecurities get the best of me."

"It's okay." She pressed her forehead to mine, just the way she used to.

Fuck, I missed this.

"I understand. I can't even imagine going through something like that..."

"It killed me." I didn't sugarcoat it. "I didn't think I'd ever get over it...until you walked into my life."

She looked into my eyes, love throbbing deep in her irises.

"You made me believe in love again. You made me believe in trust again. I guess that's why I snapped even harder—because it was so unexpected."

"I'm glad you told me," she whispered. "I wish you told me that sooner."

Did that mean we were okay?

Did I fix this?

Was she mine again?

"I do too. I guess I was embarrassed you would think less of me."

"Why would I ever think less of you?"

"Because…I should have known. I should have figured it out before I bought the ring."

"That doesn't mean you were stupid, Volt. That just means you had a good heart, and she took advantage of that. All this looks terrible on her, not you." She ran her fingers through my hair and played with the strands just like she used to. "I could never think less of you."

My hands tightened around her waist as the ecstasy hit me hard. This was really happening. She was in my arms again, and I could breathe once more. Everything was okay. I was okay.

"There's something I have to ask…but I don't want to ask it."

Just as quickly, all the feeling drained out of my body. I felt numb all over again. I had no idea what she was going to ask, but whatever it was, it wasn't good.

"How many women did you sleep with?"

How many?

So she assumed I slept with more than one.

That hurt.

"Baby, I didn't sleep with anyone." I held her gaze as I said it so she knew I was being truthful. I'd never lied to her before, and I wouldn't start now. "I know I was angry and said a lot of mean things, but I never hooked up with anyone."

"Even that first week?"

I shook my head. "There's never been anyone but you. I promise."

Her eyes softened again and she came back to me. Her arms tightened around my neck as she pulled me closer.

I wanted to know if she'd been with anyone else, but I couldn't bring myself to ask. If her answer was yes, I wouldn't be able to handle it. It would break my heart more than Sara ever did. It was better not knowing. If I didn't know, I could just not think about it. That solved my problem.

Taylor could read my mind just the way she used to. She looked into my eyes and saw the unspoken question. She answered it for me. "No." Her hand moved down my chest to the area over my heart. "When you saw me in the bar, I was telling him I wasn't interested. All I've been doing is sitting around my apartment and missing you. There's never been anyone else."

That answer was music to my ears. When I woke up that morning, I was hollow and alone. I felt like an old tree that had lost most of its leaves and bark. There was no hope in me, no desire for a better tomorrow. I returned a year into the past, bitter and hateful.

But now I was myself again.

I was with the woman I loved more than anything in this world. I worshipped the ground she walked on and wanted her for all my life. Losing her was the most painful experience of my life. And getting her back was the greatest one. "I love you." My lips moved to her forehead, and I placed a kiss there.

She took a sharp intake of breath, wincing at the contact of my lips. "I love you too."

I grabbed her t-shirt and quickly pulled it off, wanting to get this foreign and meaningless item of clothing out from between us. She allowed me to pull it off even though she wasn't wearing anything underneath. Her tits were bare but I didn't look. I pulled off my shirt and placed it over her body, covering her with the right piece of clothing. My old shirt still lay under the kitchen table, but it probably didn't smell like me anymore. "You needed an upgrade."

Instead of looking embarrassed that she'd been caught, she felt the fabric in her hands. "Thank you."

Seeing her wear my clothes was instantly a turn on. It was the most possessive way to claim her, to see my baggy clothes cover her down to her thighs. I wanted to be inside her, to feel our bodies move together, and not just because she was wearing my shirt.

I missed her.

When we made love, it brought me to a different plane of existence. Our minds intertwined together, and our hearts beat as one. There was no past and no future. There was just us—and that moment.

My hands guided her down the hallway, my face still pressed close to hers. I didn't kiss her even though I wanted to. I was saving it until the right moment, when she was on her back and her legs were wrapped around my hips. I was waiting until I conquered her, until I claimed her as mine again.

I got her on the bed and moved on top of her, our clothes still on. Her hair sprawled across the pillow and her eyes lit up in desperate desire. She wanted me as much as I wanted her, and my cock hardened at the thought. This woman was special to me in a way I could never explain.

She was my best friend, and she was the sexiest woman I'd ever laid eyes on—even when she wore her flamingo earrings. I was a man very much in love—and I didn't care if that made me a pussy.

I got her clothes off until she was stripped down to her naked skin. My clothes were kicked off immediately afterward, and I wrapped her legs around my waist. Her hips were tilted slightly, and I could feel my cock rub against her slick pussy.

I leaned over her and gave her a soft kiss on the mouth, feeling the energy coil down my spine. It spread throughout my entire body, giving me a surge that nearly crippled me. It wasn't just the physical attraction that I had for her. It was so much more than that, even though I couldn't explain exactly what that was.

Her kiss started out soft, but quickly electrified into something harder. Her small tongue entered my mouth and found mine. Together, they danced, lightly touching each other until our lips brushed past one another. She breathed hard into my mouth, my name sitting on the tip of her tongue.

I got lost in our kiss, no longer thinking about the heartbreak I'd endured for the past few weeks. Losing her once made me realize I could never lose her again. My life would turn out quite differently, and for the worst. I would have died alone while she married some other guy and started a family. My life would be a sad story of heartbreak.

Thankfully, that didn't happen.

I would never lose her again. I would hold on to her tightly and never let go. I would make her happy for the rest of my life just as she made me happy, and together, we would have something incredible.

And that started now.

Chapter Four

Taylor

When I woke up the next morning, I wasn't sure if I was really awake. It must have been a dream because Volt was right beside me, gloriously naked. His defined abs made riverbeds in his body, and he looked like someone took a knife and carved him from stone. His chest rose and fell steadily, his mind still deep in his dreams.

No, this was real.

I snuggled closer into him and wrapped my arm around his waist. He kept the chill away with his natural heat, acting as a personal heater that only I could use. The weather outside was heavy with snow, but it felt like summer inside the bedroom.

He must have felt me stir because his eyes slowly opened. He looked at the ceiling before reality came back to him and he understood exactly where he was. His hand slowly moved to mine on his stomach and he rested it there. "Morning."

"Morning." I breathed into his neck, loving his naturally masculine scent. It was better than his old t-shirts because the scent faded away on those. But with his body, it never faded away.

He rolled over and moved on top of me, his sleepy eyes telling me exactly what he wanted. He separated my legs with his arms and immediately pressed his head to my entrance. With a gentle thrust, he was inside me.

We'd hardly spoken a word to each other but we were back at it. Last night, we made love so many times I wasn't sure if my body could operate at full capacity the next day.

But it could.

He thrust into me gently, pushing through my slickness with his swollen cock. He stretched me like he always did, and it felt incredible. His was the largest size I'd ever taken. I was hesitant at first, but now I could never go back. My body loved every inch of his thickness.

His eyes locked to mine and the sleepiness slowly faded away. Desire replaced it, taking over until it had complete authority. He groaned as he felt the moisture between my legs pool for him. My body naturally obeyed his command, and my slickness grew thicker and wetter.

He groaned again, feeling the change as he slid in and out of me. Sweat collected on his back and his ass contracted as he rammed into me against the headboard.

My nails trailed down his back, feeling the muscle coil and shift. I felt power radiating underneath his skin. He was a behemoth of stranger, a beast only I could tame.

"Baby…"

I felt the explosion deep inside me. It started as a slow burn, an impending fire that was just seconds from reaching me. Flames licked my limbs before they intensified into a deep inferno. Then Volt took me into the forest fire, making me burn from the inside out. I didn't realize I was screaming because the sounds fell on deaf ears. All I could hear was the crackle of the flames as they danced.

My body felt so tender down below. As his cock slid in and out of me, it felt even better. My body was always down for multiples when it came to Volt. But I wanted him to be satisfied instead of prolonging his release until he was no longer able to control it.

"I want you to come inside me." I missed it. I missed feeling his essence sitting inside me with its weight. I missed the burn in his eyes as he deposited his seed. It was something I never found sexy before, but with him, I loved it. "Volt." I knew hearing his name was one of his triggers.

He released a quiet moan in the back of his throat as he rammed into me harder, prepared to give me everything he had.

I widened my legs and gave him ample room to shove himself inside me. I grabbed his ass and pulled him deeper into me, waiting for the grand finale.

His eyes locked to mine as he slid his entire length inside. He held his breath as the collision hit him right in his center. A moan he'd been suppressing burst from his lips as he emptied himself, giving me as much as my body could handle. "Fuck." He pressed his face into my neck as he caught his breath, still finishing.

My nails dug hard into him, turned on by the action alone. I realized it was one of my fetishes, something I loved even though other people may think it's strange. I'd never let another guy come inside me before so I'd never experienced it.

He kissed my neck then my jawline before he placed a soft kiss on my lips.

I cupped his face and deepened the kiss further, falling harder for him than ever before.

He pulled away and slowly eased his cock out of me, its semi-hard shape still coated in my wetness. His fingers moved to my lips and made sure his come wasn't leaking out. The fact that he wanted to keep it inside me was sexy in its own way.

He lay beside me then wrapped his arms around me, returning to a quiet cuddle. He faced me on the pillow we were sharing and looked into my eyes, his thoughts a mystery.

I ran my hand up his chest, feeling the strength of his muscle underneath. I loved his body because it was powerful. But I also loved it because it was his. He was the most beautiful person I'd ever seen in my life.

I treasured him.

"Can I ask you something?" he whispered.

He could ask me anything and he knew it. "Yes."

"Have you ever had sex without a condom?"

"Yes."

"Have you ever let a guy come inside you before?"

I knew what answer he wanted, and judging the excitement in his eyes, he already expected it. It was just another way to claim me, to possess me. "Just you."

His chest shivered in a growl and approval was clear in his eyes. He'd been never been jealous of my former lovers before, but that detail seemed important to him. His hand snaked up my hip until it rested at the curve of my waist. "That's really sexy."

"I like it too...not sure why."

"I know exactly why you love it so much." He brushed his nose against mine. "Because it's me."

I sighed happily when he touched me like that, in the most tender way possible. He could screw me in the dirtiest ways possible, but then he treated me like a delicate flower, something fragile that he never wanted to hurt. "I missed you so much..."

His eyes fell in sadness. "I missed you too."

"I spent all my time trying to not think about you...but that just made me think about you."

"I noticed the bedding is new...and the house is strangely clean."

"Futile attempts."

"I'm glad you didn't forget about me."

"It's not possible."

He pressed a kiss to my forehead then ran his fingers through my hair. "Every night I went to sleep drunk. Otherwise, I could never get to sleep. Your ghost kept haunting me."

I stroked his chest, feeling my pity rise.

"My parents have been hammering me about you, asking if you're coming to dinner. I didn't know what to say so I kept dodging the question. I couldn't tell them we broke up. Then it would be real."

"I didn't tell my parents either."

"At least now we don't have to," he whispered.

"So, does that mean we're going to dinner with your parents tomorrow? For Christmas?"

He shrugged. "I don't really want to go, honestly."

"You don't?" I asked in surprise.

"I just want to stay home with you. I want to make love in front of the fireplace. I want to put up a Christmas tree. I want to do all the things we couldn't do before because we weren't together."

"I think it'll hurt your parents if we do our own thing." As much as I also wanted it just to be us. "Maybe we can have a quick lunch with them or something."

"I guess." The sadness left his eyes. "No wonder why my parents like you so much. You're on their side."

"I'm not on anyone's side."

"Doesn't seem that way."

"They're excited you have a girlfriend for the holidays. Doesn't happen very often. I know my parents are sad I won't see them for the holidays."

"I'll buy your plane ticket." He said it without hesitation, wanting to give me the world on a platter.

"No, it's okay," I said. "But thank you."

"Please," he pressed. "What's mine is yours."

"It's too late now anyway. Maybe we can go see them for New Year's."

He nodded. "That's a fair compromise."

"Thank you for the offer. That's very sweet of you."

"You're my best friend. I would do anything for you."

Chapter Five

Volt

Her apartment was nice, but it was cramped. I had a spacious penthouse on the top floor of my building, and in general, it was much nicer. So we decided to shack up there instead.

I dragged the Christmas tree into the apartment and erected it by the window. I hadn't had a Christmas tree in my apartment since...actually, ever. I just wasn't into the Christmas spirit. But with Taylor, I wanted to make our first Christmas together special.

She carried the box of lights in the house and set them on the ground. "Do you need help?"

"I got it, baby." I inserted the stump into the clamp and the tree stood up tall. "Smells good."

"Yeah. It's going to look so nice with these lights and ornaments." She opened the box and pulled out the lights. "I haven't done this in forever."

"Me neither." Together, we decorated the tree with lights and ornaments. It went from a blank tree with deep green needles to a present of its own, twinkling with lights and sparkles.

She pulled her phone out. "Can we take a picture together?"

I wasn't big on pictures. It was just strange. But, I would do anything she asked. "We should." I grabbed the phone and held it out so we could take a picture together. I snapped the shot and handed it back.

"I'm going to send it to my parents. They'll be so happy." She typed a message then sent it off.

I looked down underneath the tree. "But we don't have any presents to put underneath...besides the one I got Clay."

"That's fine," she said. "That's not what Christmas is about."

I grabbed the present I got Clay and placed it under the tree.

"That was nice of you to get him something."

"He's a good kid." I cared about him more than I could put into words. He didn't feel like a friend or a student. He felt like a son to me, even though I was too young to really understand how that felt. "I hope he has a good Christmas." Taylor and I never saw eye-to-eye on this matter. She still thought I should have involved social services and had Clay removed from his home, but nothing had happened since I beat the shit out of his father. He was close to getting out of there anyway.

"Me too." She didn't venture into the argument because she knew it wasn't the time.

"Now what?" I took off my jacket now that we were inside. It still had flecks of snow from the blizzard that raged outside.

She eyed the fireplace in the wall. "Does this work?"

"It's not just for show," I teased.

She shot me a half assed glare.

"I can start it up if you want."

"If you don't mind. Maybe we can lie in front of the fire." Her cheeks reddened and her thoughts gave her away.

"That sounds like the best Christmas Eve I've ever had." Just a few days ago, I thought I was going to spend it drunk off my ass. Now, I was happy again. It was so disconcerting it was hard to believe. "But I do have some bad news." I walked to the wall and flipped the switch. "It's gas."

"You have gas?" she asked with a cringe.

"No, the fireplace," I said as I rolled my eyes.

She saw the gas flames burn through the glass, deep blue and purple. "Oh…"

"But it'll still be warm."

"And romantic." She gathered a few blankets and pillows and set up everything on the floor. She placed an air mattress next to the fireplace so we wouldn't have to lie on the hardwood floor. "This looks cozy."

I stripped down to my boxers then got under the covers. All the lights in the apartment were out except the Christmas lights on the tree. Flames burned behind the glass, and heat escaped through the vent.

Taylor lay beside me in just her panties and bra. I preferred her naked, but when small articles of clothing covered her body, it looked extremely sexy. Her tits were pushed together in the fabric, showing off that bombshell figure.

My cock was hard in my boxers, just as it was anytime this woman was near me. We made love several times already, and I didn't want to ruin the tender moment by immediately going for sex.

She cuddled beside me and ran her fingers down my chest. Her nails slowly dragged into my skin, scratching me in the same way she did when we made love. The scent of vanilla and oranges washed over me.

I loved that smell.

"There's nothing better than being tucked inside on a winter day while a sexy stud keeps you warm."

"Sexy stud, huh?" My fingers glided through her hair, feeling the soft strands.

"Oh yeah."

I didn't get her anything for Christmas because I hadn't thought about it during our break up. I was too depressed to participate in the Christmas spirit. While everyone else ran around getting gifts for people, I moped around in my apartment. I was too depressed to even order from Amazon. "I wish I had a gift to give you…" It was our first Christmas together, and we had nothing but an empty tree.

"It's okay," she whispered. "We don't need gifts when we have each other." She moved on top of me and a strand of hair escaped from behind her ear. It fell onto my face, hitting me right in the nose.

I tucked it back and let my hand linger on her cheek. I watched the stars sparkle in her eyes before I inched her face closer to mine, planting a soft kiss on those sexy lips.

My hand migrated behind her back, and I unclasped her bra, feeling it come loose against my chest. Her tits peeked out, perky and round. She had the nicest tits in the world. I couldn't wait to slide between them again. It was something we needed to do more often.

Her boobs brushed against my chest as she moved. They were soft, even the nipples, and I loved feeling them drag across my body. There was nothing sexier than feeling a woman press up against me like that. It made my cock twitch in anticipation.

She straddled my hips and dug her nails into my stomach like it was the rein on a horse. She vibrated her hips against me, dragging her wet pussy against my length. Her juice lubricated me, preparing me to enter her hard.

She was the sexiest woman I'd ever been with— hands down. She had confidence that was enjoyable to watch. She loved making me feel good because she got just as much pleasure out of it as she did when I made her feel good.

She rocked her hips back and forth, teasing me. Her eyes locked to mine, and her hips shook with every thrust she made.

She was making me wait. What a brat. "Baby..."

She rocked into me harder.

"Don't tease me." My cock was already irritated it wasn't inside her, stretching her wide.

She grabbed the base of my cock and pointed the tip at her entrance. Slowly, she slid down, taking me all the way until I was balls deep. She moaned when she had all of me, and her nails dug into me like blades.

This was the best Christmas ever.

I grabbed her hips and guided her up and down, feeling the air mattress shake underneath my body. Her hair bounced on her shoulders, and her tits shook every time I thrust into her.

"Merry Christmas."

I groaned as I felt her slickness. I slid between her lips with ease because she was so wet for me. "Merry Christmas."

***

Taylor fell asleep on my chest, her small body rising and falling steadily with each breath I took. Her hair was sprawled out across my skin, tickling me slightly with every move she made.

I ran my hand up her back, feeling the tiny muscles of her frame. Her waist was petite and her back toned. I loved touching her, exploring her in ways I never had before.

The Christmas tree twinkled from the corner of the room, the lights reflecting off the golden ornaments that hung from the branches. It filled the room with the scent of pine, smelling like a lush forest. The fire in the hearth crackled and popped. It was a night I wouldn't forget, the kind that was magical because we made it so.

A knock sounded on the door.

I flinched at the noise because I wasn't sure who would come knocking at that time of night. My watch said it was almost midnight—and it was Christmas Eve. It could be one of my booty calls, but they still thought I was in a relationship. Who else would it be?

Unfortunately, Taylor woke up at the sound. She rolled off me, her eyes drooping with sleep. "Is someone at the door?"

"Yeah."

"Are you expecting anyone?"

"No." Now I really didn't want to answer the door. What if it led to bullshit that would ruin our night together?

The knock sounded again.

I sighed in annoyance then quickly threw my clothes on. "I'll see who it is." I walked to the door with my hands balled into fists, irritated this person was so needy. I threw the door open without bothering to check the peephole.

Clay stood on the other side, bundled up in a thick jacket, the only one he owned, and a beanie.

"Clay?" He was the last person I expected to see on my doorstep at this time of night. "Is everything okay?"

He pulled off his gloves then wiggled his fingers, willing the life to come back into them. "Is it cool if I crash with you tonight?"

"Yeah, of course. Come in." Now that Clay was there, I forgot about Taylor. When it came to this kid, I didn't think about anything else. My entire focus was on his wellbeing.

He walked inside and stripped his jacket away then removed his muddy boots.

That's when I realized Taylor was still naked under the sheets in the living room. "Uh, wait right here, okay?"

"Alright," he said as he kept undressing.

I walked into the living room and saw Taylor getting dressed. "It's Clay."

"Is he alright?" She buttoned the top of her jeans and straightened her shirt.

"Not sure." I turned back around and walked into the entryway. "So, what's going on, buddy?"

He looked at the ground as he spoke. "My dad has been...drinking a lot tonight. Nothing has happened recently, but I can tell something bad is going to happen. I thought it was best I left. Normally, I would sleep in the park, but it's too cold. They say it's the coldest night of the year."

Sleep in the park? He did that normally? "I'm glad you came here."

"I figured you wouldn't mind."

"Of course not." I tempered the rage behind my eyes, irritated this kid had to spend Christmas Eve like this. And what kind of child sleeps in a park? He deserved a roof over his head and a place where he felt safe.

Taylor entered from the other room, her hair fixed and the sleep gone from her eyes. "Hey, Clay."

"Hey, Taylor," he said automatically. "Sorry, I didn't know you were here." He gave me a pointed look, wanting an explanation.

Silently, I told him I would explain later.

"Well, I'm going to bed. I'll see you in the morning." She gave me a quick kiss before she walked down the hallway and entered my bedroom. The door shut quietly behind her.

I knew she didn't want to leave. She just wanted to give Clay and me some privacy. He liked Taylor, but I was the only person he trusted. "You probably want a hot shower, huh? Thaw out those bones."

"I'm okay," he said. "Honestly, I'm starving."

Of course. How could I be so inconsiderate? "You're in luck because I'm a pretty good cook. How about grilled cheese and tomato soup?"

"That sounds bomb. I'm so hungry I'd get it out of your garbage can right now."

It wasn't funny because I knew it was true. "Coming right up." I went into the kitchen and whipped him up a hot meal. I made it extra cheesy and crispy and threw the soup in the microwave. When I was finished, I set everything on the kitchen table.

Like he hadn't eaten in a week, Clay inhaled everything. He had crumbs and soup stains all over his mouth but didn't seem to notice.

"Have you been buying lunch every day?" I gave him enough money to get through the holiday break since we weren't supposed to see each other. I hoped he was using it.

"I got mugged at the subway station."

"Why didn't you just ask me for more money?"

"Because I'm not doing that," he said with a mouthful of food. "That's lame."

"That's not lame," I argued. "I would much rather give you more money than let you starve."

"It's my fault. I should have been more aware of my surroundings."

"Clay, no," I snapped. "That criminal chose to mug you. He knew what he was doing. Don't blame yourself."

"Either way, you already do a lot for me, and I'm not asking for anything else."

"But I don't mind. Don't you get it?"

"Well, I mind. I'm not your kid. I'm not your problem." He finished his food then pushed the plate way. "Thanks for dinner."

"Yes, you are my problem. Because I love you." I've never told him that to his face before because it was implied in everything I said and did. But he needed to hear it. He wouldn't have been there on Christmas Eve unless he felt insignificant. "You always have me. I've told you that so many times, but you never believe me. When have I ever let you down?"

He propped his elbows up on the table. "Never."

"Never," I repeated. "Please come to me when you need help. If you really don't want to take money from me, fine. But come here and get some food. My fridge is always full of groceries."

His voice came out quiet, defeated. "Okay…"

Hopefully, I got through to him. "So…your dad was drinking?"

"He always drinks, but tonight was really bad. It was all hard liquor. He started knocking things over, and I knew things were only going to get worse. So I climbed out my bedroom window and took off."

"I'm glad you came here." He always had a home with me.

"Thanks…"

"Did he hit you?"

"No."

"Do you think he would have?"

He shrugged. "I'm not sure. And now I'll never know."

I hated this. I hated the fact this kid was a nuisance to everyone. He didn't have a home to feel safe in, and he didn't have any resources to make a better life for himself.

He couldn't even get food. What would've happened if we'd never met? What would Clay do? "You'll spend Christmas with me?"

"No, it's okay. I'll leave in the morning."

"Clay," I pressed. "I'm inviting you to spend Christmas with me."

"I don't want to ruin your holiday. I already crashed your Christmas Eve."

"You wouldn't be ruining anything. You would be making it better."

He didn't meet my gaze, not believing me.

"I've got an extra bedroom, a PlayStation, and plenty of food. Plus, I could use the company."

"It sounds like you have company."

"Yeah," I admitted. "But she wants you to stay too."

"I doubt it," he said darkly.

"Really, she does. She cares about you as much as I do."

"Yeah?" He finally looked at me with hesitation in his eyes.

"Yeah."

"Well...if it's okay, I'll stay."

"It's more than okay, kid." I grabbed his shoulder and gave him a gentle squeeze. "This is your home whenever you need one."

***

When I went to bed, Taylor was still awake.

"Is he okay?" She sat upright in bed, wearing one of my t-shirts.

I stripped down and got under the sheets beside her. "Yeah, he's fine. He's spending Christmas with us."

"Did his father hurt him?" she demanded. "Because I'll march over there and beat the shit out of that motherfucker myself if he did."

Whoa.

Mama bear.

Damn, she had a mouth.

"No, he didn't hurt him. Clay said he left before things escalated. Who knows what would have happened if he'd stayed."

Her eyes narrowed, her anger coming out like an explosion. "A child shouldn't have to run away from his home because he's scared. He shouldn't have to sleep on a fucking park bench. It's absolutely unacceptable."

"I know." I wouldn't argue about any of that.

"Volt, you need to—"

"I know." I knew what she was going to say, and I didn't need to hear it.

She stared at me, watching every expression on my face.

"But it can wait until after the holidays."

"It can't wait a day longer. It needs to be taken care of now."

"Look, Clay is going to be pissed at me. He doesn't want to go to a group home—"

"It doesn't matter what he wants—"

"Listen to me." I kept my voice calm so the argument wouldn't escalate higher. "Let him have a good holiday with us. Let him relax. Let him take the SATs after the New Year. And then, I'll take care of it."

She stared at me coldly, not satisfied with that plan.

"If I do it now, he won't take the SATs. He'll be so pissed off at me, he won't take the exam just to spite me. I know him."

Her nostrils stopped flaring.

"When he's done, I'll handle it. I'll sit him down and tell him what's going to happen. He'll hate me forever, but I agree with you. It's not safe for him. Apparently, his dad has forgotten the little conversation we had."

Her anger disappeared altogether. "Thank you."

"I'm not doing it for you. I'm doing it for him."

She rubbed my arm gently, her affection coming back. "I know that will be hard for you."

"It will." But I couldn't handle Clay living there anymore. He clearly wasn't safe, and I didn't want him to sleep on a park bench either. That kid deserved a better life. "He'll hate me."

"He will," she whispered. "But one day, he'll thank you for it."

I wasn't so sure about that.

She kissed me on the cheek. "You're a good man, Volt. I'm so lucky to have you."

My heart melted at the affection in her words. I loved being blanketed with her love. It was the nicest feeling in the world. "I'm the lucky one, baby."

***

"Merry Christmas, baby," Mom said over the phone. "I'm so excited to see you today."

"Merry Christmas," I said. "I'm excited to see you too."

"I got Taylor the cutest gold earrings. They'll look fabulous on her."

We were exchanging gifts? "She'll love them."

"I'm making your favorite pie so please come hungry."

"About that...there's something we need to talk about."

"Oh? Everything alright?"

"I was wondering if I could bring an extra person. I'm sorry it's last minute, but it just worked out that way."

"Oh, sure. Is it a friend from work?"

"Uh, not quite."

"Well, there's always room for one more."

"It's actually one of my students that I tutor. He doesn't have anywhere to go for Christmas, and I don't want him to be alone."

"Oh...a child?"

"He's not really a child. He's in high school."

"Is he...one of *those* kids?"

I rolled my eyes at her ignorance. "No. He's a great kid. He's being tutored for the SATs."

"But why doesn't he have anywhere to go for Christmas?"

"He comes from a broken home. His dad is a drunk, and there's no one else in the picture."

"Oh...and you think it's best if he comes over here?"

I knew my mom wasn't a bad person. She just wanted to make the holiday perfect for everyone. That was her specialty, making roasted ham with chestnuts, having a glorious fire burning in the hearth while we opened gifts in carefully wrapped presents. "Mom, it's okay if you'd prefer if he didn't come."

She breathed a sigh of relief.

"But where he goes, I go. We'll stay at my place and watch old movies and drink hot cocoa. It'll be fun."

"What?" she shrieked. "But you have to come over. I have to see my baby on Christmas."

"I'm sorry, Mom. But I need to be with Clay."

"Then of course he can come."

"Mom, I don't want to step on your toes. Really, it's fine."

"Nonsense. You better be over here in an hour or I'm going to hunt you down and drag you over here. Got it?"

I pinched the bridge of my nose in frustration. "Are you sure?"

"Yes."

"I want Clay to feel welcomed."

"He will, baby. I promise."

"Then we'll be there."

"Oh, thank god. You almost gave me a heart attack."

"Sorry about that. Not a good way to start Christmas."

"I'll see you soon, baby. Love you."

She really needed to drop the 'I love yous' every chance she got. "Love you too." I hung up and walked back into the living room. Taylor and Clay were watching TV, still wearing their pajamas. Clay borrowed my stuff so I could wash his filthy clothes. "Everything is set."

"Really?" Clay asked. "They don't care that I'm coming?"

"Nope," I answered.

"Are you parents nice?" he asked.

"Look at me. They must be awesome if they raised a guy like me."

Clay rolled his eyes. "They're freaks, aren't they?" He left the couch and walked toward the bathroom. "I'm going to shower."

"Alright." As soon as I heard the door shut, I turned to Taylor. "We've got fifteen minutes. Let's have some Christmas sex in the bedroom."

"What?" she asked incredulously. "With Clay in the house?"

"He's in the shower."

"That's still weird."

"What? He knows what sex is."

"But he's a minor. It's unacceptable."

"Oh, come on." I leaned over her on the couch and pulled one leg around my hip. "You want me to take you right here?"

She pressed her hands against my chest. "Don't be nasty."

"But I want to be nasty." I brushed my lips past hers. "I want Clay to feel welcome here, but I'm not giving up my sex life for him. So, let's have a quickie."

The playfulness jumped into her eyes. "How quick are we talking?"

"Consider it a race. I'll see how quickly I can make you come."

***

Clay fell silent when we reached the front door. His hands were deep in his pockets and he looked uncomfortable. He scanned the area around us, looking for an escape route.

I placed my arm around his shoulder. "They're gonna love you."

"You think?" he asked.

"Definitely. My mom is always excited when people come over. She lives for it."

"She won't think I'm…" He looked down at his old clothes and his jacket with holes everywhere. "I'm a bum?"

"No. My parents will love you." I patted him on the back before we walked inside.

When my parents heard the front door open, they rushed to the entryway. "Merry Christmas!"

"Merry Christmas," Taylor and I said together when we saw them round the corner.

They didn't blink an eye over Clay's appearance. In fact, they went to him first. "Merry Christmas, Clay. We're so excited to have you here. We have cookies, pie, and gifts. My name is Sherry." Instead of extending her hand to shake his, she pulled him in for a hug.

Clay stood still, frozen in shock. "Thank you…"

When Mom pulled away, Dad hugged him next. "Hope you're hungry. We have way too much food and not enough bellies."

"Thank you for having me over," Clay said politely. He never exercised manners around me, but he used them now. He wanted to be a good guest, and I knew he was doing that for me.

"Of course," Dad said. "A happy house is always full of people."

My parents hugged and kissed me next, suffocating me like they hadn't seen me in years. My cheek had Mom's lipstick smeared on it, and Dad almost crushed my ribs when he squeezed me.

When they moved to Taylor, they were a lot gentler. They gave her soft embraces and treated her like she was a fragile piece of china.

Why didn't I get that kind of greeting?

***

We had dinner together at the table, and Clay sat beside me. He watched every little thing I did, copying the way I held my knife and fork. He tried to cut his meat the way I did and mimic me so he wouldn't stick out like a sore thumb.

79

Mom sat across from him and pretended not to notice him struggle with the utensils. "So, you're taking the SATs soon?"

"After the new year," Clay said. "Volt has been helping me every day after school."

"That's nice of him," Mom said. "Volt is a pretty smart guy. He learned from the best." She nodded at my father.

"He's the nicest guy I've ever met." Clay looked down at his food as he ate.

I smiled to myself, treasuring the rare compliment.

"He's pretty nice," Mom said. "And he got that from me."

"I think Clay is going to do really well on the exam. We just finished algebra the other day, and he nailed it." I sipped my cider and ignored the bottle of wine Mom placed beside my glass. I didn't drink around Clay because of his experience with alcohol. I never wanted him to feel uncomfortable around me.

"Wow," Dad said. "That's the most difficult part of the test."

"I think he's going to get a great score and get into a good school," I said. "We're hoping for something local, maybe a state school."

"Well, a letter of recommendation from the principal at Bristol Academy would probably help." Dad winked at Clay.

"Thanks," Clay said quietly.

It meant a lot to me that my parents were working so hard to make Clay feel welcomed. I'm sure it wasn't easy for them to let a young stranger into their house on the most special day of the year, but they did it for me.

After dinner, we gathered around the tree to exchange gifts. On the way there, I quickly bought a few things for my parents since I'd forgotten to do that sooner. Thankfully, the mall was open on Christmas.

Actually, it was kind of sad.

To my surprise, my parents had more gifts for Clay than anyone else. They stacked the presents beside him, wrapped with the same meticulous perfection as all the other gifts.

Clay stared at them in shock. He didn't open any of them, like he wasn't sure if they were really for him.

"Open one," I said from my seat beside him on the floor.

"Uh, these are all for me?" he asked in surprise.

"Of course," Mom said. "Go ahead."

"You didn't need to do that..." Clay looked down, embarrassed.

"We wanted to, sport," Dad said. "That's what Christmas is all about."

I knew Clay was uncomfortable with all the attention. He accepted it politely up until that point, but now he reached his limit. I stepped in to relieve the tension. "What's in this one?" I grabbed one present and shook it. Something rattled inside, but I couldn't tell what it was. "Hmm..." I ripped off the wrapping paper and revealed a Nerf gun. "Wow. This thing is sick." I flipped over the box to read the back instructions. "Damn, this thing shoots fifty miles an hour."

"Hey, no cussing," Clay teased.

"Whoops." I shrugged. "And it comes with ammo. How sick is that?"

Clay took the box from me. "Wow. That is awesome."

"Now I have to get one so we can start a war."

"I'd kick your—"

"Butt," I finished for him. "And no you wouldn't."

"We'll see about that. We'll take this to the park tomorrow."

"You're going down."

Clay opened the rest of his gifts once the tension had been dispelled. My parents got him a ton of stuff, from different toys to a new jacket that would keep him warm through the harsh winter. I wasn't sure how Mom bought all that on short notice, but when it came to Christmas, she was superwoman.

Taylor put on the earrings Mom got for her, and they glinted from the lights on the Christmas tree. "Thank you so much. I love them."

I whistled. "You look cute in those."

Taylor blushed and looked away, aware that my parents heard everything I said.

Like I cared.

We continued exchanging gifts until the floor was covered with wrapping paper. Piles of trash were everywhere, and even a huge garbage bag couldn't contain everything.

"Wow, that was a great Christmas, Mom." I said that every year, but I meant it every time.

"Thanks." She beamed with pride, accomplishing the mission she spent all year prepping for.

"That was the best Christmas I've ever had," Clay whispered, looking at all the presents he collected. He was too embarrassed to meet anyone's gaze. "Thanks for everything."

"Aww…" Mom's eyes watered.

Dad smiled, growing fond of Clay just the way I did.

Taylor got teary-eyed too.

Mom moved from her place on the couch and wrapped her arms around him, giving him a maternal hug he'd never received before in his life. This time, he returned the hug, letting someone actually hold him.

Now I really dreaded what I was going to do after the holidays were over. I was going to do something Clay trusted me not to do, and it would hurt our relationship. It might break it altogether.

And I might lose him.

Chapter Six

Taylor

The following morning, I woke up before Volt. On his days off, it was impossible to get him out of bed. Sometime, he would lie there until after ten.

I, on the other hand, got grouchy when I didn't eat first thing in the morning. I needed something in my stomach, even if it was just a banana, so I went into the kitchen to search his pantry.

Clay was already awake, playing a video game. The tree was still lit up and the fireplace was still going. All of Volt's clothes looked a million times too baggy on him because he was skin and bones.

"Morning, Clay." I brewed a pot of coffee.

"Morning." He hit the buttons frantically as he concentrated on his game.

"Hungry?"

"Sure."

I found a few things inside Volt's fridge and whipped up pancakes, bacon, and eggs. The sound of the sizzling pans and the smell of the warm food must have woken up Volt because he came down the hallway a moment later. He wore his sweatpants low on his hips and didn't bother with a shirt.

"Morning, baby." He wrapped his arms around me from behind and kissed my neck.

"Morning. But go put on a shirt."

"Why?"

I lowered my voice. "Clay is in the next room."

He rolled his eyes. "That kid lives on the streets. He's not going to care."

"I don't think it's appropriate."

"What? You don't like to see me walk around shirtless?"

"That's not what I said..."

He snatched a piece of bacon and took a bite. "Crispy."

I finished the pancakes then set the table. "Breakfast is served."

Clay threw down his controller and practically ran to the table. "Sick." He rubbed his palms together greedily before he helped himself to the food. He slathered everything in syrup and scarfed it down like someone might take it away from him.

"Hungry?" Volt teased.

"It's just really good," Clay said with a mouthful.

"My lady knows how to cook." Volt rubbed his leg against mine under the table. "What are you playing?"

"Call of Duty," he said.

"Which one?"

"Black Ops."

"Cool. That's a good game."

Clay was wearing some of the new clothes Volt's parents got him. After a shower and a change of clothes, he was a handsome kid. If he just gained a few extra pounds, he would look like every other kid, someone with a house and a family.

"You want to stay with us until school starts up again?"

"No," Clay said quickly. "I'll leave today. I don't want to cramp your style."

"You aren't cramping our style," I said. "We love having you around."

"It's okay," he said. "If I were in an apartment with a cute girl, I would want to be alone too..."

Volt chuckled. "We really don't mind, Clay. We actually wanted to see if you wanted to go ice skating with us."

"Ice skating? What the hell is that?"

"You've never been ice skating?" I guess I shouldn't be surprised since there were a lot of things he hadn't done.

"No," Clay said. "I'll pass."

"Want to go to the arcade?" Volt asked.

"Hell yeah," Clay said. "I love that place."

Volt and I just got back together, and I didn't want to share him with anyone. I wanted us to lay around the house all day and look into each other's eyes. But I knew Clay needed him more than I did. "I need to exchange Christmas gifts with Sara, so I'm going to do that this afternoon."

"You aren't going to come with us?" Volt asked.

"You guys will have more fun without me. Besides, I have a lot to tell Sara." She didn't know Volt and I got back together, and that was a long story.

"You're sure?" Volt asked.

"Absolutely." Clay deserved to be pampered for once in his life. All I really wanted was to sleep with Volt. When the door was locked and the lights were out, we did the things I craved the most. I got to have him—in every way possible.

Volt saw the truthfulness in my eyes and dropped the questions. "Alright. We'll be home later."

She unwrapped her present and screamed. "Oh my god! Where the hell did you get these?" She held up a pair of Gucci stilettos.

"Well, I got them at an outlet store when they were on sale. Plus, it was black Friday. And I had a gift card. Not to mention, I sold my soul to the devil."

She hugged them to her chest. "Oh my god, they are the cutest things ever."

"I'm glad you like them."

"I'm so wearing these to work next week. My ass is going to look off the hook."

"Hopefully, it lands you a cute guy. And a rich one who can afford all your expensive taste."

"I don't have expensive taste," she argued. "I just have classy taste."

If you say so.

"Now open yours." She handed over the box.

I ripped it open and found a white gold necklace with a set of charms in a separate box. Each one had a different safari animal. There was a giraffe, a parrot, a rhino, and a hippo. "Wow. This is so cute." I loved it. I would wear it to school every single day. I slid the charms on before I clasped it around my neck.

When I saw it, I thought of you.

I felt the charms in my fingertips, knowing Volt would get a kick out of it. "I think we did a pretty good job this year."

She hugged her shoes again before she placed the box in the chair beside her. "I love Christmas."

"What did you do?"

"Went out with some friends. Couldn't get the time off to fly home. My parents were upset, but they'll get over it."

"It's a long flight." When we went to Washington for Thanksgiving, my ass was flat for days from sitting for so long.

"And expensive. So, what did you do for Christmas?"

Now was the best part of the conversation. "I spent it with Volt."

She stared at the grin on my face, still confused. "Meaning?"

"We got back together."

"What?" she blurted. "What happened to never taking him back?"

"Well...he gave me a good justification for his behavior. After that, I couldn't stay mad at him."

"What was his excuse?"

I'd guard his secrets just as much as I guarded hers. "It's personal. But trust me, it made perfect sense."

"How do you know he didn't just make it up?"

"He hinted at it earlier in our relationship, but never talked about it. Besides, he wouldn't lie to me."

"Did he sleep with anyone else while you were apart?"

"No."

"Are you sure? He could have lied about that."

"He wouldn't lie to me. If that's what he said, then that's what happened."

"I don't know...three weeks is a long time to be single."

Now she was just pissing me off. She didn't know Volt the way I did. She hadn't even met the guy. "I trust everything Volt tells me. He wouldn't lie to me just to save his ass. If that's what he said, then it's the truth."

"Okay, sorry." She leaned back, picking up on my hostility.

"Why aren't you happy for me?"

"I am happy for you. But...never mind."

"No, tell me."

"You don't want to hear it. And if you're happy, just keep being happy."

Now that the tension settled in the room, I couldn't ignore it. I needed to know her thoughts. We told each other everything since we were little. Men weren't immune to that. "I want to know."

"Are you sure?" she asked. "You aren't going to yell at me?"

"I didn't yell in the first place."

"Okay, fine." She leaned over the table again. "From what you said about him, it seems like he has anger issues."

"He flipped out, I admit that. But it was one time."

"But he really flipped out and said some unforgiveable things."

"I know."

"It just makes me wonder if he's emotionally unstable."

"He's fine."

"But are you sure?" she asked. "He seriously went off the deep end. He turned into a man you didn't recognize. If this happened once, who says it won't happen again."

"It won't happen again. And if it does, I'm gone."

"I don't know…" She shook her head gently. "It took so long for you two to get together, and not long after you're together, you break up. It just sounds like the two of you aren't compatible. I'm sure he's hot and has a nice cock, but maybe you need someone a little more tame."

There was no one else for me besides him. I understood how it looked to an outside point of view. Sara hadn't met Volt and didn't understand all the ways he was so blindingly romantic. She didn't know about his sweet relationship with Clay. She only saw one sliver of him, a sliver that didn't do him justice. I loved Sara like a sister, but she wasn't as open-minded as I was. Once she settled on an idea, she stuck with it, stubborn beyond reason. "Volt is a lot more than a nice cock. The package underneath is what I care most about. It's the part of him that I fell in love with. We hit a rough patch, like all couples do, and I don't think that means I should just turn my back on him. I believe in him. And he believes in me."

Sara held my gaze, not flinching under my heated stare. If she were uncomfortable, she hid it well. She pressed her lips tightly together while her eyes remained glued on me. Then she leaned back into the chair again, surrendering. "Fine. You know what you're doing."

I do know what I'm doing. "Please keep an open mind when you meet him."

"I'm not as catty as you think I am."

"Yes, you are. And we both know it."

She rolled her eyes. "If you love this guy and you're going to fight for him, then he must be special. I want you to be happy, so I'll behave myself."

That wasn't enough. "I want you to like him, Sara."

"I said I would be nice to him and keep an open mind. I'm not going to like him unless he gives me a reason to. So, he better step up his game because I'm a tough audience."

"So be it."

***

Volt and I enjoyed our winter break together but it wasn't as magical when a third person was always around. Clay did everything with us. Stuck to Volt's side like his new best friend, they went everywhere together.

And he slept over every night.

I didn't mind having him there because he was a good kid, but I hated being silent as a mouse when we

94

fooled around. When he made love to me, he kept his moans in the back of his throat. I had to shut my mouth and use my nails to express my feelings. I ended up scratching him and nearly making him bleed. He had marks all over his skin but didn't seem to care. I had to remind him to wear a shirt around the house so Clay wouldn't see my claw marks.

By the end of the two weeks, I knew Clay had to leave. And I was dreading it. Because when he left, Volt had to do the right thing and contact social services.

As the days drew closer, he became tenser. The fear was deep in his eyes. He didn't want to go against Clay's wishes, but there was no other option. He lay in bed beside me, not in the mood for sex like he usually was.

I lay beside him and ran my hand across his chest. I tried to comfort him in the only way I could. My fingers weren't enough, but at least it was something. "It'll be alright."

"He'll hate me."

"In the beginning, but he'll understand eventually."

"No. He'll just hate me."

"Give him more credit than that."

"You don't get it," he whispered. "I'm the only person he has. I'm the only person he trusts. If I do this, he'll see it as a betrayal. He'll look at me differently. I know exactly how he thinks."

"I'm sure he'll come around eventually."

"I'm afraid it'll make it worse. I'm afraid he won't go to college just to spite me."

"No. He wouldn't have come to you in the first place unless he wanted to pursue a better future."

"But he's emotional. He'll shut down if he has to. It's a defense mechanism to him."

"Talk to him first. Maybe that will ease the blow."

"Yeah…but I have a feeling it'll just make it worse."

"Why don't you get social services involved but never tell him you were the one behind it?"

"Clay isn't stupid," he snapped. "He'll figure it out. And I'm not lying to the kid."

I leaned over his chest and pressed a kiss to his ribs. "It'll work out, Volt. Don't worry about it."

"How can I not worry about it?" He was immune to my kisses. "I know I'm important to him, but he's also important to me. I don't want to lose him. He means a lot to me."

"I know…" I rubbed his chest. "And he knows that too."

"But will that be enough?"

"It will." I pressed more kisses to his chest, trying to soften him up and redirect his thoughts. I wanted to fall in the throes of passion so he wouldn't think about anything else.

His hand moved into my hair, feeling the strands fall through his fingertips. "At least I have you to get through it." His fingertips brushed against my cheek, feeling the soft skin. Longing flared in his eyes, telling me how much he adored me.

"You always have me."

He pulled me onto his chest and forced my legs to straddle his hips. "I like it when you ride me. Feels good."

"Yeah?" I grabbed his large length and directed it at my entrance. I was wet without even realizing it. I slowly slid down, stretching apart as I took him.

His hands gripped my ass and pulled me down his length. Once he was completely inside me, I felt his cock swell further, enjoying how wet and tight I was. "Ride me, baby."

I couldn't move fast and hard like I wanted. I could only lean over him and give him slow strokes. His cock gently slid into me, moving until his length was completely sheathed. He rocked into me from underneath, slowly moving.

He propped himself on his elbows and tilted his head back, kissing me as I moved harder. When his mouth was clamped over mine, it silenced my moans. I breathed harder into his mouth as I took him over and over.

"You're the best sex I've ever had."

I stopped moving and kept my face pressed to his. Was that just a line? Or did he actually mean it?

He read the question in my eyes. "I mean it." He thrust his hips up, wanting to keep going.

I got swept away in the pleasure, and I kept riding him as he made me feel everything from the sun to the moon. I felt the explosion rise over the horizon, hitting me with more rays until I completely ignited in flames.

He grabbed my ass and pulled harder onto his length, digging deeper into me. He was about to come, about to follow me into the pleasurable abyss. He moaned into my mouth before he hit his trigger, releasing deep inside me. He loved claiming me like this.

And I loved being claimed.

***

A week went by and school started up again. When my students filed into my classroom, it was obvious they didn't want to be there. By the end of the week, they still didn't want to be there.

Neither did I.

I wanted to marry Volt and be his full-time sex slave. That sounded so nice. It probably came with good hours, good pay, and excellent benefits. When we got married someday, I hoped he would be down with it.

That Saturday was the SAT session that Clay signed up for. We agreed to drive him to the campus and wait outside until he was finished. It was a long test, taking up to five hours.

We waited inside Volt's apartment for him to arrive. It was early in the morning, about seven. No one should up that early on a Saturday.

It should be against the law.

Volt wasn't affectionate with me while we waited. He kept to himself, his nerves getting to him.

"You're worried about how he'll do?"

"He knows the material. I'm not worried about that." He leaned against the counter with his arms across his chest. He wore a dark blazer that molded to his shoulders perfectly. His chest fit tightly against it, the outline of his pecs visible through the fabric of his shirt.

"Then what are you worried about?"

"That he'll get nervous. That he'll panic. That he'll see all the smart kids and start to question himself. That he won't be able to focus."

"I'm sure he'll be fine."

"Even if I could just sit in there with him, I'd feel better."

"Maybe you can."

"I don't know. I guess I could ask. Just having me in there might make him more comfortable. But then again, every student would want their parent nearby so that wouldn't be fair."

"Unless you say you're there for some kind of research for your company."

"Hmm...that's not a bad idea."

"It's worth a shot."

Clay knocked on the door.

Volt opened the door and fist-bumped Clay. "Ready, man?"

"I think I got this," he said with a shrug.

"You're going to do great." Volt wrapped his arm around Clay's shoulder. "You've got this in the bag. We'll go to Mega Shake afterward to celebrate."

"Hell yeah," Clay said.

We got into Volt's fancy car then drove across town until we found the university where the exam was being administered. Clay ate his breakfast on the way there, something Volt packed for him.

After we parked the car, we walked him into the building.

"I've got it from here," Clay said.

"It's a big place," Volt said. "Let's make sure you get there on time without any problems."

We found the registration counter and checked Clay in before we stood in line to enter the auditorium.

"I'll be right back." Volt walked away, probably to check with someone about sitting in.

I stayed with Clay, seeing his body tense with anxiety. He kept shifting his weight back and forth, eyeing the other kids around him. "I don't see anyone from my school."

"They might be in a different room."

"I'm the only poor kid here..."

"What does that matter?" Volt was right when he said Clay might tense up. "When you submit your application to college, that doesn't matter at all. You're going to do great on this test. It doesn't matter what your clothes look like or how much you have in your wallet." I pressed my finger against his temple. "All that matters is what's in here." I pointed to his chest. "And there."

He rolled his eyes. "That was so cheesy."

"But true."

Volt returned, a disappointed look on his face.

I silently asked for the outcome with just my eyes.

He shook his head.

The doors opened and people started to file in.

"Alright, here we go." Volt placed his hand on Clay's shoulder. "Just relax and do your best. There's no pass or fail. There's just a raw score."

Clay nodded.

"I know you're going to do great." Volt did something I'd never seen him do before. He wrapped his arms around Clay and hugged him. "No matter what that test score is, I'm so proud of you."

Clay hugged him back, pure emotion coming into his eyes. "Thanks for everything…"

"You're welcome." He pulled away and ruffled his hair. "Now go kick some ass."

Clay smiled. "Does that mean I can cuss now?"

"When you walk out of that exam, you can drop as many F bombs as you want."

He chuckled. "You're going to regret saying that."

***

Volt couldn't sit still, not even for a second. He paced in the hallway and kept eyeing his watch. The exam seemed to stretch on forever. I suddenly felt bad for putting my students through gruesome finals. How did they expect anyone to pay attention for that long?

"Do you think he's okay?" Volt ran his hand through the back of his hair, sounding like a concerned parent at the doctor's office. He kept pacing back and forth, crossing his arms over his chest then running his fingers through his hair again.

"He's fine. Sit down."

He shoved his hands into his pockets but continued to stand there.

It was sweet that he cared so much for Clay. Seeing their relationship grow and change right before my eyes was a privilege. Volt had the biggest heart in the world.

When he told me he lacked compassion and love, I knew that was a lie. He had more love to give than anyone else I'd ever met.

"Volt?"

"Hmm?"

I grabbed his arm and pulled him onto the bench beside me. "You've been tutoring him for almost a year now."

"Yeah."

"And do you think he learned a lot?"

He nodded.

"Do you think he has what it takes to do well?"

He nodded again.

"Then have some faith. That kid is tougher than he looks. He's going to concentrate and do amazing. You'll see."

Volt stared at the floor before he finally came to his senses. "You're right."

"I know I am." I rubbed his arm and rested my head on his shoulder. "Clay was taught by the best. He'll do great."

He turned his head my way and placed a kiss on my forehead. "I've always cared about my students but with

Clay, I feel something else. I can't explain it. I just want the best for him—in everything."

"You love him."

"It's more than that. When I'm not with him, I worry about him. When he's hungry, I feel sick inside. When he's scared, I want to die."

"Maybe you see him as a son."

"I do. But I'm not old enough to be a father."

"That's not true." He was over thirty. Lots of people had kids before they were even twenty.

"But I'm not old enough to be the father of a teenager preparing for college. He's exactly half my age."

"That doesn't mean he can't see you as a father figure. He looks up to you. You can see it in his eyes."

"Well...yeah."

I continued to rub his arm. "I feel that way about my students sometimes. I do the best I can in class, but sometimes, I wish I had them a little longer. I wish there were more hours in a day so I could teach them even more new things. I wish I could help them every time they needed me."

"At least you understand me." He moved his hand to my thigh, giving it a gentle squeeze.

105

"Hopefully, Clay will go somewhere local so you can still see him all the time."

The mention of the future immediately killed Clay's spirit. He wasn't thinking about college because he was thinking about tomorrow.

"What if we tell him I'm the one who called social services? I am a teacher, and I have an obligation to report stuff. You could pretend you didn't have a clue."

"That's nice of you to offer, but it won't work. Clay will know. He's a smart kid." Volt bowed his head, unable to hide his unease. True love was measured by the hard things, not the easy things. Volt could look the other way and continue being Clay's best friend, but he knew that wasn't the best thing for him. Despite the heartbreak it would cause, he knew what he had to do.

I tried to change the subject to lighten his sad mood. "Sara is eager to meet you." That was a borderline lie, but it didn't change what would come to pass.

"Oh, yeah. Forgot about her."

"After you meet her, you won't be able to forget her."

"Did you tell her about our break up?"

I nodded.

"Great...she thinks I'm an ass."

"No, she doesn't. I told her we got back together, and all she wants is for me to be happy."

"Yeah...she hates me."

"Remember what you said to me about your parents?"

He stared at me blankly, not having a clue what I was talking about.

"You told me it wouldn't make a difference whether they liked me or not—because nothing would change us. That same idea applies to Sara. If she didn't like you, I won't care."

"But she's your best friend."

"So? That doesn't mean I agree with everything she says."

"It's easy to defy my parents. But it's not so easy to go against your friend's wishes."

"It's easy for me."

He returned his hand to my thigh. "Thanks..."

"Of course." I kissed him in the corner of the mouth. "Besides, who else is going to give it to me as good as you do?"

He grinned, liking that comment. "You have a point there."

"I love what I've got, and I'm not going to look for some elsewhere."

"Good thing I'm an excellent lay."

"And a sweet man."

The doors opened, and the kids filed out. Most of them looked exhausted, tired of concentrating for five hours straight. Others just seemed happy that the exam was over and done with.

"He must be starving," I said. "I can't go an hour without eating."

He chuckled and stood up, taking my hand in his. "I know how that is. My wallet suddenly felt lighter when we started dating."

"Hey, I offer to pay for things."

"Baby, you know I'm joking."

Clay emerged out of the crowd, and he didn't seem relieved that the test was completed. In fact, he looked worse now than he did when he first walked inside.

"Hey, man." Volt clapped him on the shoulder. "How'd it go?"

"Okay," he said with a shrug. "I put down your address for the exam score. That's cool, right? If it was sent to my house, my dad would see it and—"

"Yeah, that's cool," Volt said. "We can look at the scores together when they get there."

"Okay," Clay answered. "Thanks."

"Now tell me about the exam." Volt walked on one side of him, guiding him through the hallway and back to the parking lot.

"It was long." Clay rubbed the side of his temple. "Like, it gave me a headache."

"They should give them breaks," I argued. "How are they supposed to function under all that pressure?"

"I don't know," Volt answered. "It wasn't like that when I took the exam."

"It wasn't like that for me either," I said.

"Were there questions you had no idea how to answer?" Volt asked. "Or did you recognize everything?"

Clay shrugged. "I don't know...there were a lot of questions."

"Volt." I came to his side and hooked my arm through his. "Stop interrogating the poor boy and let him relax. He's probably starving and needs to pee."

Clay chuckled. "Listen to your girlfriend."

Volt backed off and gave him some space, hooking his arm around my waist. "Mega Shake is still good?"

"Dude, I'd eat your face right now," Clay said. "That's how hungry I am."

"Then let's get there quick," I said. "Because I really love Volt's face."

***

Clay ate slower than he usually did, probably too tired to scarf down his food. He ordered a soda and a milkshake, totally burned out from answering three hundred questions.

Volt didn't interrogate him again, but it was obvious it was a struggle to hold himself back. He shook his leg underneath the table, taking out his impatience on himself. He was normally smooth and suave, but when it came to Clay, he was a different person. He reminded me of my father, constantly protective and overbearing.

It was cute.

"Clay, do you know what kind of job you want to have?" I asked. Up until that point, Volt had never told me what Clay was interested in. He only mentioned he wanted to attend college.

"Not sure," he said with a shrug. "All I know is I don't want to sell drugs."

I didn't react to his words even though it took all my strength not to. He came from a different world, one I would never understand. "Any reason to pursue higher education is a good one."

"I just don't want to end up like my dad. You know, drunk and high all the time. Most days, he doesn't know what's going on. His life is meaningless. When he dies, no one is going to care or notice."

"So, you want to make a difference?"

"I guess," he answered. "I just want to make enough money to have my own place, somewhere that I can be safe. I want to have food on the table and never worry about where my next meal is coming from. Maybe get a car or something."

This conversation reminded me how much I took for granted. I didn't grow up rich, but I was certainly never afraid of missing my next meal. I was never afraid my parents would smack me around. It was easy for me to say my childhood was happy. "I think that's great. There are a lot of ways you can make money and be happy."

"I don't like math, so I don't want to do anything involved with that."

I chuckled. "Math can be tough. What's your favorite subject?"

"English. I like reading and writing. Well, I do now. Before, I hated it."

"Maybe you can be a teacher. Or maybe a writer."

"Maybe," he said. "I hope I figure it out when I'm at college. I'll go to a junior college for now then transfer."

"Why not go to a four-year right off the bat?" I asked.

"Because I won't get in." He said it simply and with no pity. "But that's fine. I've heard of kids doing it that way. Apparently, it's cheaper too."

"Smart kid, huh?" Volt said. "He really thinks about things." Pride was heavy in his voice.

"He is smart," I said in agreement.

Clay looked down, avoiding our gaze when the attention became too much.

"Mr. Rosenthal?" A man in a crisp black suit walked up to the booth. He had dark brown hair, bright blue eyes, and he looked to be in his early fifties. A woman was beside him, also brunette. Judging the way they held hands, they were married.

"Hey, Mr. Preston. How are you?" Volt rose to his feet and shook his hand.

"I'm great," he answered. "Just thought I would come over and say hi. I hope that software has been working for you."

"It's been great," Volt answered. "My tutors use it with the kids, and it really helps. Thanks for the donation."

"I'm glad to hear it." He turned to the woman who must be his wife. "This is my wife, Scarlet. Baby, this is one of my clients."

Volt shook her hand. "It's a pleasure to meet you. Your husband is a great man."

"Thank you," she said with a pretty smile. "Why do you think I married him?"

Mr. Preston looked at her with a familiar gaze. It reminded me of the way Volt look at me. The love throbbed from deep within him. It was unmistakable. He turned back to the conversation, his eyes falling on me. "Is this the special woman you were telling me about?"

He talked about me?

"Yep. This is my lady." He pulled me to a stand and wrapped his arm around my waist. "Taylor."

"It's so nice to meet you." I shook hands with both of them.

Mr. Preston eyed Clay. "I didn't know you had a son. I have two kids but they're out of the house."

"He's not my son," Volt said quickly. "But pretty close. He's one of my students, Clay."

Clay waved as he sipped the last of his milkshake.

"Well, it was nice seeing you." He secured his wife to his side as they walked out. "Take care."

"You too." Volt waved as they walked past the window before he turned back to me.

"I know him from somewhere..." I'd seen his face before but I couldn't remember where I saw it. It sounded like he worked in technology, which was far away from my profession.

"He's Sean Preston," Volt explained. "One of the Preston brothers."

I was still drawing a blank.

"Even I know who he is," Clay said as he finished his fries.

"You've seen his face on TV and magazines," Volt explained. "You just don't remember it."

"I guess so. I didn't realize you were cool with famous people."

"Well, I'm a pretty cool guy." He flashed me that playful smile before he sat down again. "So, you better stick with me."

"Well, I was going to stick with you anyway."

He pulled me onto his lap. "Good. We'll be sticky together."

I glared at him when he made the dirty joke in front of Clay.

"What?" Volt asked. "The kid is sixteen. He's not stupid."

Clay stopped eating his fries, a cringe overcoming his face. "He's not hungry anymore either."

Chapter Seven

Volt

I was procrastinating.

Big time.

It was worse than not doing a paper that was due in a week. It was worse than not writing up the exam the night before it was supposed to be given. I was putting this off because I had no intention of doing it.

Clay would hate me.

He would see it as an act of ultimate betrayal.

And I couldn't blame him. I told him I wouldn't throw him under the bus and now I was going against my word. Everything was fine until his father stepped out of line. Nothing happened, but something could have easily gone wrong. Clay was gone for nearly two weeks, and his dad didn't seem to care.

What kind of parenting was that?

Maybe if I sat Clay down and had a serious talk with him, he would understand. He would see that I was trying to help him, not hurt him. He was a smart kid and had come a long way. Surely, he would understand I was just trying to do the right thing.

But in my heart, I knew he wouldn't.

A week went by and I still didn't make my move. I had all the contact info I needed to get Clay started in the process. I researched the different orphanages he would be staying at, and while none of them were the Ritz, they seemed tolerable.

Taylor didn't mention the situation, even though it hung heavy in the air like a rain cloud. But her patience was waning. If I didn't do something soon, she would give me an earful about it. She loved Clay just as much as I did, and every day he stayed in that hell hole was a day too long.

After work one night, I made dinner for the two of us. I made parmesan chicken with spaghetti, something so easy a monkey could do it. I didn't usually eat a lot of carbs because it quickly affected my size, but I'd been craving it. Plus, Taylor loved Italian food.

"Wow. Everything looks great." She sat across from me and rubbed her palms together. The wind she made with her hands traveled over the candle and made it flicker. A distant glow fell on her cheeks, making her them rosy and her eyes sparkle.

"Thanks." I passed the tongs so she could help herself first.

She served the spaghetti onto her plate and grabbed a piece of chicken. "Have you ever cooked for anyone else?" She poured herself a glass of wine then placed the napkin on her lap. Her words lacked any sort of jealousy.

"Not for my flings," I answered. "But I did for...my last girlfriend." I hated ever admitting I was in a relationship with that whore. She blinded me and made me immune to my surroundings. She tricked me into a false sense of security. How many other people knew she was sneaking around? Did everyone know?

"How long were you with her?"

I didn't like talking about her. She didn't deserve my memory. "About a year."

"And you were going to propose to her?" she asked in surprise.

Yes, it made me look bad. "I thought I was in love." The whole thing made me look like a pussy.

"Were you in a relationship before her?"

"Not really. I would be with someone for a few months before we went our separate ways. She was my first serious relationship."

Taylor nodded as she kept eating. "I know it's not the same thing, but I feel like what I went through with

119

Drew was similar. I never loved him, but I was pretty hurt he played me so easily. That's why I never confronted him about it. That would have let him win."

"Yeah…" I never thought about it before. The situations were similar.

"So, when she broke your heart, you went on your sex rampage?"

"Yeah. I told myself I would never fall in love again. I would never have another relationship. I would never let someone play me like that. It wasn't just painful. It was embarrassing."

Her eyes softened as she stared at me across the table. "No one thinks less of you for that."

"No?" I asked. "You should."

"How so?"

"A girl only looks around for someone else if she's unsatisfied. Apparently, I wasn't satisfying." But after sleeping with more women than I could count, I fixed that problem. I met a lot of interesting women in my travels, and I had a lot of sex. I got out of my comfort zone and tried new things. I did the bondage thing, the roleplaying thing, and everything else you could think of. All that experience made me a behemoth in bed. Women kept coming back for more.

"Or maybe there was something else going on. You said the guy was her ex, right?"

"Yeah." Why the fuck were we still talking about this?

"Maybe they ran into each other and old feelings surged. Maybe it was just a kiss and only a kiss."

Doubtful.

"I just don't think you should necessarily attribute her actions to your inadequacy."

"If she was truly happy with me, she wouldn't have messed that up for a quick kiss—with a man she's already kissed." I dug into my food and kept my eyes down, wanting her to stop with the questions. I couldn't call her out on it since I screwed up our relationship just a few weeks ago. None of that would have happened if I had just been honest with her.

"I know you don't want to talk about it. I can see it in your eyes. But, I can't let you keep thinking you were the problem."

I looked at her again, seeing the softness in her eyes. "You weren't there. You don't know."

"But I do know. You're the most amazing man in the world, Volt. She was the one with the problem, not you."

"Well, thanks for saying that, but now we'll never know."

"So, all that sleeping around was just to get better in bed?"

"Partially," I said. "And just to feel good. It worked for a long time until you showed up. The warmth you carried with you made me realize how cold my life was, how empty it was. And that's when I decided to give love another try."

She held her utensils in her hand but didn't take another bite. "What happened to this girl?"

I shrugged. "I have no idea. I never kept tabs on her. I never cared to wonder what she was doing with her life."

"You never ran into her?"

"Nope." Thank god.

"I can't even imagine that..."

I sipped my wine. "What?"

"She cheated on you and thought she got away with it. I wonder if she went back to her ex and they're still together."

"Maybe." I didn't give a damn.

Taylor finally dropped the conversation, sipping her wine quietly. Now that she asked everything she could possibly ask, we should never have a reason to talk about Sara again.

She was finally buried.

"For what it's worth, I think you're absolutely amazing in bed."

I stopped eating because the sentence took me by surprise. I didn't need her to tell me that. It was obvious in the way she came around my dick and begged for more. It was clear by the look in her eyes when I rocked into her. Everything she did and said made it abundantly obvious. "I know." After spending a year of my life fucking everything that moved, I became an expert on the female anatomy. I knew what women wanted, how they wanted it, and what kind of fantasies they held. I was grateful I could apply this knowledge to the one woman who actually mattered. "And you're amazing too. The music we make together is hypnotizing."

"You can say that again." She went back to eating her dinner, having barely touched it. We spent so much time talking that neither one of us really got to eat anything. We fell into a quiet conversation about work and her students.

We wiped our plates clean then finished the rest of the wine. Together, we usually went through a whole bottle. Taylor couldn't handle her liquor as well as I could, but when it was just her and I, she didn't care how much she drank. I was getting her into bed either way.

"Volt?"

"Hmm?"

Her eyes drooped from alcohol, desire, and exhaustion. "You need to talk to Clay."

I knew this moment was coming. She held her tongue for a week but the alcohol made it loosen.

"Every night he stays in that house is another night where he might not come out alive. Volt, you need to look after him. By doing nothing, you're guilty."

"I know."

"It's been a week, and you haven't made a single move."

"I know…"

"Talk to him or I'll step in. I hate to step on your toes and pressure you, but this kid is important to me. We have to look out for him. We can't drop the ball on this."

She repeated herself enough times. "Okay."

"When are you going to talk to him?"

I wanted to say next week but that answer wouldn't suffice. It would have to be sooner than I wanted. "Tomorrow."

I hoped tomorrow would never come.

***

Now that the SATs were finished, Clay wasn't being tutored every day like he used to be. We only met once a week to go over his homework and help him with any additional questions he had. Since we started working together, his grades had picked up significantly. Two of his teachers called me just to ask how I managed it.

I told them I didn't do anything. Clay did all the work.

Clay met me in the conference room like usual, and he sat across from me with his homework and the details for his science project. We'd become closer than ever before, having a relationship based on a deep foundation of trust, respect, and love.

I didn't want to lose that.

Taylor wasn't the only person who fixed me. Clay made me realize I wasn't a selfish asshole like I once thought. He made me realize I still had the capacity to love when I thought it was lost. He made me realize I needed a

125

family someday. That was something I couldn't live without. He brought out the best in me—and chased out the worst.

"I'm glad you and Tayz are back together," Clay said. "I like her."

"I like her too. And what did you just call her?"

"Isn't that her nickname?" he asked. "She told me that's what her friends call her. It's catchy."

If she was cool with it, then I was cool with it. "Yeah. She's pretty fantastic."

"Are you going to marry her?"

A question like that would have made me snap in anxiety months ago, but now I was eerily calm. "If she'll have me."

"When are you going to ask?"

"Not sure. Haven't thought about it."

"Well, chicks like her don't come around very often. You should put a ring on it before it's too late."

"We haven't been together very long." Maybe a few months if you took out the breakup.

"But weren't you kinda together when you were just friends?" he asked.

He remembered more than I gave him credit for. "Yeah."

"So, doesn't that count?"

"It's debatable."

"I think you should go for it."

"Since when did you become the love doctor?" I asked with a smirk.

"I'm not," he argued. "But I think if you find someone who really makes you happy, you shouldn't let them go. Remember what you were like when you broke up? I do. God, you were annoying!"

A laugh escaped my chest. "Annoying?"

"Yeah. You were moping around all day and licking your wounds. You were a pain in the ass."

I didn't berate him for the curse word. When he said stuff like that, it made me fonder of him.

"I hate to say it, but you were a huge pussy."

"I was." I wouldn't deny it.

"And if a girl can whip you like that, then she's the one."

"I see your reasoning."

"So, let me know when you're going to ask."

I wasn't in a hurry, but I also hated going back and forth between our apartments. I hated the nights when she went home because she had laundry and cleaning to do. I hated the fact we weren't together every second of the day. I never grew tired of her, and when she wasn't around, I didn't know what to do with myself. "I will."

Clay turned back to his book. "I'm supposed to do a science project, but I don't know what to make. Is the volcano with baking soda and vinegar too cliché?"

It was the most cliché thing in the world. "Yeah."

"Yeah, you're right." He stared across the room as he tried to brainstorm.

I came to a dead-end in the road and knew I couldn't move any further. The time had arrived, and I had to drop this bomb on Clay and hope for the best. Hopefully, he would see reason and understand I just cared about him. I wasn't working against him like everyone else. "Clay, we need to talk about something..."

"What?" He looked up. "Did my test scores arrive?"

"No, not yet." I closed his books and stacked them on the side of the table.

He watched me, fear coming into his eyes. "Okay..."

"This isn't easy for me to say. Keep an open mind, alright?"

"Uh, I'll try."

"After what happened on Christmas Eve, I can't let you stay there anymore."

The words sunk into his skin, and the realization slowly entered his brain. His eyes changed from friendly to sinister. "What the fuck is that supposed to mean?"

"Clay, your father is dangerous, and he could hurt you."

"He already has, and I'm fine. Why are we talking about this? I told you I'm okay staying there. I don't want to leave."

"But one of these nights, he might kill you."

"Maybe. But I doubt it."

"It shouldn't even be a possibility," I argued. "Don't you see that?"

"Look, this is the hand I was dealt. It's not that bad. I'll be out of there soon."

"But—"

"I knew I shouldn't have gone to your apartment. I should have slept on a park bench."

"No. You can come to me for anything and you know that."

"Not if you're going to rat me out." He shook his head. "I knew I couldn't trust you. I should have kept my goddamn mouth shut."

This was taking a turn for the worse, and my heart started to ache. "Clay, I wouldn't know what to do with myself if I lost you. I love you like my son, okay? I can't handle someone hurting you."

"Whatever," he snapped. "I've been okay for this long. I'll be okay for a little longer."

"But you deserve more."

"I'm not going to an orphanage," he snapped. "Word will get out at school, and everyone will tease me more than they already do. I'll be the stupid kid with no parents. I'll be the stupid kid that has a drug addict for a father. What kind of chance do you think I'll stand in a place like that?"

"It won't be as bad as you think it will."

"Volt, it's my life. Maybe I'm not an adult yet, but I should have a say in what happens to me. I don't want to go there. I've taken care of myself for this long. Why don't you trust my judgment?"

"I do trust your judgment, Clay. But remember, I'm the adult. I have a lot more wisdom than you. I wouldn't make this suggestion unless I thought it was the best thing for you."

"Well, you don't know what the best thing is for me," he snapped. "You don't know anything with your perfect family and your perfect house. You guys had more food to eat than I've had in an entire year. You guys sit around and talk because you have so much free time. We come from different worlds. I know my world a lot better than you do, so stop acting like you understand. You don't and never will."

"Clay—"

"Shut up," he hissed. "If you tell anyone, I'll never forgive you. I'll never speak to you again. I'll hate you for the rest of my life."

My eyes stung when he said those words. Nothing hurt as much as that. I was devastated when Taylor left me, but this was a new kind of anguish.

"Friends don't do this to each other. I'm directly telling you what I want but you aren't listening."

"Clay, I have to keep you safe."

"By ruining my life?" he hissed.

"It won't be as bad as you think it is."

"And you know because…?" He leaned forward, growing more vicious. "Do you have any idea what social services is like? Do you have any idea what an orphanage is like? I have friends who've gone down that road. I know things that you never will. So stop acting like you understand. You don't get it."

"I know you're afraid of change—"

"I'm not afraid of change. I'm afraid of losing my freedom. I'm afraid of losing my rights. Maybe my dad is a drunk and a drug user, but he leaves me the fuck alone. He does his thing, I do mine. I come and go as I please."

"Because he doesn't care about you."

"And that's fine because I have you."

Somehow, that hurt even more.

"But if you do this, I'm going to lose the one person I actually thought cared about me."

"I do care about you."

"Then drop this bullshit now."

I wanted to duck my head and cower but I couldn't. This was hard—even more difficult than I anticipated. Clay was persuasive, and I almost gave in to him. I almost did what he asked. But I had to straighten my backbone and lay down the law—no matter how much it hurt. Clay couldn't live in that place for another year. If he did, he would wind up dead. "Clay, this is what's going to happen. I'm calling social services tomorrow and explaining everything to them. They'll investigate the situation. You can lie all you want, but they'll take my word over yours. When they come to the house, they'll see it's an inhospitable environment anyway. Then they'll proceed from there. I'm sorry this isn't what you want, but this is what's going to happen. I'm telling you now so you can be prepared."

Clay stared at me, his hands shaking on the table. The anger buried behind his eyes was about to explode. Rage pumped in his blood, and he was just a second from leaping across the table and attacking me. It was the kind of ferocity he couldn't contain.

I held my ground, hating myself more with every passing second.

Clay jumped up and snatched his things. He threw his backpack over his shoulder and walked to the door.

"Clay." I rose to my feet, not wanting things to end like this.

He turned around, his hands still shaking. "I trusted you. I fucking trusted you and you stabbed me in the back.

You're just like everyone else. You think you're better than me, smarter than me, know better than me. But you don't get it and you never will. I hate you, Volt. I fucking hate you and never want to see your piece-of-shit face again. Fuck off." He stormed out of the conference room and slammed the door shut behind him.

I watched him walk away through the windows, hearing his words echo loudly in my head. It was like the echo inside of a seashell. It would last forever, continuing on endlessly for my own turmoil.

I dropped back into the chair because my legs no longer worked. My body shut down because it couldn't handle the shock that just rocked me. My eyes watered with tears I didn't think I could ever possess. I was broken beyond repair, my heart shattered in two. I just lost someone who meant the world to me and now he hated me.

Despised me.

I leaned over the table and rested my face in my hands, feeling the hot tears bubble to the surface of my eyes. I tried to fight them back. I couldn't remember the last time I cried. It must have happened when I was a child. But now I couldn't contain my depression. I was sick to my stomach with pain. My body ached like I'd been tortured.

And the tears came.

***

Taylor came over after work, a bag of groceries in her hand. It was her turn to make dinner.

I forgot she was coming. I forgot everything about my life after my conversation with Clay. Nothing else seemed to matter, even the woman I was madly in love with.

"Work was such a snore." She set the bag on the counter. "The students had an exam, so I surfed the web on my computer all day long." She put the groceries away, depositing the vegetables and meat into the fridge. "How was your day?"

I leaned against the wall, unable to hold my body up.

When I didn't respond, she turned to me. "What's—" She stopped talking when she saw the tortured look on my face. My despair radiated like a beacon, and my entire body was just a shadow of what I used to be. I didn't need to say anything to explain my feelings.

She knew.

"Volt..." She wrapped her arms around me and held me tightly, allowing me to bury my face in her neck. She ran

135

her hands up and down my back, holding me up with her small stature.

Feeling her body next to mine combated the pain but didn't eradicate it altogether. It was a small respite from what I was feeling, but nothing in the world could make it disappear altogether. "He hates me."

"No, he doesn't." She continued to comfort me, to love me in the greatest way possible. But no amount of love could erase what I just lost. Nothing could bring Clay back to me.

"Yes, he does."

***

After a lengthy conversation with the school and social services, everything moved forward. They conducted their investigation, and based on what they found at Clay's apartment, it was grounds for his immediate removal.

I expected Clay to run away as soon as we had our conversation, but he didn't. Maybe he thought I would change my mind. Maybe he thought saying he hated me would be enough to steady my hand.

Nothing could have changed my mind.

I took a backseat to the investigation since I was merely a witness, but I knew the drill. I knew what would come next. It was only a matter of time before Clay was placed in an orphanage. He wouldn't go into a group home since those were designated for at-risk youth. Clay may look like a problem child but his grades and SAT score said otherwise.

My life was a blur at that point. I went to work and stayed in my office most of the time, having meaningless meetings and phone calls. My only client no longer needed my services, so I was left to my own devices.

My job suddenly felt insignificant.

When I went home at the end of the day, Taylor was there. She took care of me, cooked for me, and rubbed my back until I fell asleep every night. Without her, I wasn't sure what I would've done.

I didn't give her the attention she deserved but she didn't seem to care. She was too concerned about me to care about herself. Sex was off the table, and I was a terrible conversationalist. The two of us usually sat in silence in front of the TV. Sometimes she graded papers or worked from her laptop, but having her there was a comfort.

I couldn't go through this alone.

"He's in an orphanage now." I got the news from the social worker that took on the case. When she told me the news, I was relieved and depressed. Now Clay was safe. But he was also miserable.

"Which one?" she asked.

"St. Anthony's."

"I heard that one is nice."

"Yeah…"

She rested her hand on my thigh and rubbed it gently.

"Maybe I should go see him tomorrow. Do you think he'd see me?" I hated how weak I'd become. I hated how pathetic I sounded. Everything that defined me as a man disappeared once Clay hurt me.

"I think you should give him more time. Let him get used to the orphanage before you stop by."

"Yeah?"

"Yeah. It's going to take him a while to get used to it. If you go right now, he'll just be angry. Maybe in a few weeks he'll like it and his opinion will change."

"Hopefully."

She patted my thigh. "How about some dinner? I made lasagna."

"Not hungry." I hadn't been eating. My appetite disappeared, and I already lost weight. My body couldn't handle the lack of nutrients and protein to uphold my size.

But I didn't care.

"I'll put it in the fridge for later." Taylor never pressed me on anything. She did what I asked without complaint. She was a trooper through the whole ordeal. If and when I snapped out of this, I'd have to thank her for everything.

"Okay."

She left my side and walked into the kitchen where I couldn't see her anymore. The second she was gone, I felt like shit. Being alone, even for a moment, was enough to rip me apart.

***

I agreed that going to the orphanage was a bad idea. At least right now it was. He was bound to hate it just the way he claimed, and seeing me would just unleash a flood of fury.

But I still wanted to see him.

I walked to Cunningham High School and stayed on the opposite side of the street. I wore jeans and a t-shirt with a Yankees baseball cap. I never wore hats unless I was at a game, but it was the best way to shield my face.

The bell rang, and the kids filed out of the building. They walked across the lawn in groups, talking to their friends as they decided what to do with their free time.

A moment later, Clay walked out alone. His old backpack hung from his shoulders, and he kept his head down like he didn't want anyone to notice him. A group of kids walked by and one threw his empty soda can at Clay's head. "Loser."

It took all my strength not to cross the street.

I wanted to tell that kid off.

But since I wasn't Clay's father or a teacher, I was just a strange man that didn't belong there. And that's the kind of stuff you went to prison for.

Clay reached his bike and took it out of the rack, not fazed by what just happened. He didn't seem to care at all, like it happened on a regular basis.

That hurt even more.

He walked his bike to the sidewalk then swung his leg over the side. From a distance, he looked exactly the same. He wore the same clothes and did his hair in the same way. But his eyes looked different. They were stripped of hope, just empty chasms of nothingness.

He pedaled the bike down the sidewalk and crossed the street, leaving my gaze once he disappeared behind a building. He was going the opposite way of his apartment.

Even though he was gone, I stayed there because I had nowhere else to go. I should be at work with Clay sitting across from me. But now I was back to my former life before Clay stepped out of that elevator.

I was back to being nothing.

Chapter Eight

Taylor

I hated seeing Volt like this.

He was heartbroken.

It was the only way to describe that look on his face. He lost someone he cared so much about, and now that Clay was gone, he wasn't sure what to do with himself. He loved him more than he could put into words. While trying to do the right thing, he lost him.

I wished I could fix it.

Volt was unnaturally quiet, having nothing to say anytime we were together. He communicated with me by using his eyes, showing his overwhelming despair. He was drowning in his own sorrow and there wasn't a life jacket in sight.

All I could do was be with him. Sit beside him. Hold his hand. Let him know he was never alone. That I would carry the burden with him—silently. I went to his place every day after work and made dinner and did his laundry. I slept beside him every night even though I never got any action.

I knew my presence comforted him.

He didn't need to tell me.

After two weeks, his sadness didn't change. He was still a shadow of what he was once before. His reactions were either slow or non-existent. He hardly responded to the sound of his own name—and that was something he loved to hear.

There was nothing I could do to fix his pain. Only person held that power.

And that was Clay.

***

I checked in at the front desk then proceeded to the game room. It's where the kids hung out before dinnertime. Some of the younger kids were playing with their toys on the ground. The teenagers sat on couches listening to their headphones or scrolling through their phones. A lot of them looked at me with irritation, hating the fact I walked into their personal zone.

Clay sat in the nook by the window, his head leaning against the cool glass. He played with a pocketknife in his hands, running his thumb along the blade. He looked just as lifeless as Volt.

I came to his side and watched him, waiting for him to acknowledge me.

He pretended I didn't exist.

"Clay?"

"Hmm?" He looked out the window.

Did he even know it was me? "Hey. I just came by to check on you."

He finally looked at me, and for a split second, he seemed happy to see a familiar face. Memories of our time together flashed across his eyes. But then it disappeared instantly, replaced by a steel wall of indifference. "I'm fine. You can go now." He returned his gaze to the window.

I pulled up a chair and sat beside him, knowing I had to play by his rules if I wanted to accomplish anything. "Have you made any friends?"

"Just enemies."

"How's the food?"

"Tastes all the same to me."

"Do you have someone to help you with your homework?"

"This place is understaffed and we're oversaturated. Hell no, I don't have any help in here."

His pain hadn't dwindled in the past two weeks, and his heart was just as hard as the day he walked out on Volt. "Volt really misses you."

"I don't care."

"He thinks about you all the time."

"Good for him."

"He thinks you hate him."

"I do," he snapped. "I meant every word I said. He stabbed me in the back. I couldn't care less about him."

"I know you don't mean that."

"Then you don't know me."

"You know, in your heart, he did this to look after you."

"Bullshit."

"Clay, look at me." I had to get through to him. I had to make this right for Volt. I couldn't stand by and watch the man I loved fall apart.

"I'm good."

"Please," I whispered.

He finally turned to me, loathing in his eyes.

"You're more lucky than you realize."

"Yeah?" he asked sarcastically. "Because I'm not a starving kid in Africa? Yeah, I've heard that one before."

"No. You're lucky you have someone in your life that's willing to do anything to help you. You're lucky Volt loves you so much that he did something he didn't want to do. He knew you would hate him. He knew you would break his heart. But he put you in here anyway because he knew it would keep you safe. Now, that's real love. Maybe one day you'll see that."

He shook his head. "He betrayed me."

"He gave you one chance to stay there. If nothing had happened, you would still be there. But Volt's message to your father wasn't enough, and he settled into his old ways again. He gave your preference a chance before he went with the alternative. Clay, I know you're smart. You can't sit there and tell me you don't understand his point of view."

"I do," he answered. "But he still should have stayed out of it. I may be sixteen but I know how to survive. He shouldn't have stuck his nose where it didn't belong. I stuck out my neck in need of help, and he did the one thing he promised not to do. I took a chance on him when I shouldn't have."

"It's not that bad here, Clay."

"Oh, really?" He nodded toward two older boys on the couch. "They're the crimson twins. You know why they're called that? It's not because crimson is their last name."

I shuddered at the thought. "If anyone in here gives you a hard time, just tell someone."

"And then get a worse beating for being a snitch?" he asked incredulously. "When the lights go out and we're in bed, shit goes down. Volt thinks I'm safe in here? I can't run away. I can't go anywhere. When things get tough, I have to stick around. He may think he helped me, but he just made my life a million times more difficult."

Reconciliation seemed impossible at this point, but I couldn't give up. Volt needed this to be fixed. He need Clay's forgiveness—as well as Clay himself. "I know this is—"

Clay hopped off the nook. "I'm tired of this. Goodbye, Taylor."

"Clay, wait."

He walked down the hallway and entered a room. The door shut behind him, and he never came back.

I stayed in the chair and looked out the window, wondering if I made things better or if I made them worse.

***

I didn't tell Volt about my visit with Clay. Since nothing good came of it, there was no reason to inform him. Besides, it would just make him more miserable anyway.

I made dinner like I did every night. He had two bites, and then I stored it in the fridge for the next day. Volt was hardly eating, and his muscle definition was beginning to soften. I didn't care if his body changed, but I did care that he wasn't healthy.

How did I fix this?

We went to bed that night, cuddled together under the soft sheets. I usually lulled him to sleep by caressing him, running my fingers through his hair or down his chest. It was the only way he would drift away. Otherwise, his regrets would consume him alive.

Tonight, I wanted things to be different. I wanted to bring him back to life, to pull him from the brink of death. He was fading fast and losing who he was. He was fading from vibrant to a dull gray.

I moved on top of him and straddled his hips, hoping he wouldn't reject me.

He looked at me, his usual arousal absent.

I pulled my shirt off and tossed it on the floor. I wore nothing underneath, and my tits were on display for him to enjoy. I knew he loved my chest most of all. He played with boobs every chance he got. They were proportionally big in comparison to my size, so they looked perkier than they really were.

I ran my hands up his chest, grinding against the area where his hard cock would be. I was just in my black thong, trying to entice him to take me. I leaned over him and sprinkled kisses against his five o'clock shadow. My nipples rubbed against his chest, pointed.

"Baby…"

I was getting to him, making him melt. He was coming back to me.

"I'm just not in the mood right now." He grabbed my shoulders and pulled me back. "I'm sorry. It's not you."

I failed.

I was rejected.

I tried not to let the sting bother me because it wasn't personal.

"I'm sorry," he repeated.

"Volt." I returned my hands to his chest. "You can't stay like this forever. It's been weeks now."

"I know."

"Come back to me."

"It's just hard for me to be excited about anything anymore. I keep thinking about what he said to me…that he hates me."

I leaned over him and cupped his face with a single hand. "He'll come back to you. I know he will."

"I don't know…"

"He will. I promise. But you need to give it time."

"Time seems to be all I have."

"Come on." I grinded against him, trying to get him hard. I never dealt with this kind of rejection before and it stung. But I had to remind myself it wasn't about me. His inability to get a boner stemmed from his depression.

"You really are beautiful." His hands snaked up my thighs to my ass. "I don't know what's wrong with me."

"Just don't think about it." I leaned over him and gave him a slow kiss, easing him into it. I sucked his bottom lip before I dove my tongue into his mouth, dancing with his. I rubbed his chest at the same time, wanting him to understand how much I wanted him. This dry spell was killing me. Just doing this was about to make me come.

I breathed into his mouth as I kissed him. "I want your big cock inside me. I want my man to make love to me. I want him to fill me…"

His cock sprung to life and pressed against me.

I never thought I could pull off dirty talk, but with Volt, I could do anything. "You feel so good..." I rubbed my clit against him, feeling my body light on fire. Having this kind of intimacy hit me in the right spot. "Fuck, I'm so wet."

He moaned into my mouth, getting into it. His fingers kneaded my ass, gripping my cheeks tightly and pulling them apart. Two fingers curved around my ass and felt my entrance. He rubbed the moisture onto his fingertips and moaned quietly, confirming what his dick wanted to know.

He quickly rolled me over onto my back and dominated me with his large size. Now that his sexual need had awoken, he realized how much he desperately needed it. He hadn't gotten laid in weeks, and his cock was starving. He pulled my underwear off and sank deep inside me. "Fuck."

I gripped his shoulders and clawed into his back. "I'm already going to come." I wasn't embarrassed by how quickly it happened. I had to lay beside him every night for weeks without making a move. It was pure torture.

"Baby..." He thrust into me hard, giving me powerful strokes that stretched me wide. Not having me for weeks affected him the same way it affected me, even if he didn't realize it until now. He pinned me farther into the mattress, giving it to me harder and deeper.

"Volt, I'm going to come."

He moaned as he thrust into me. "Me too."

"I want your come inside me." I grabbed his ass and pulled him deeper into me. I was on the precipice of a powerful orgasm, the kind that would ignite and consume me.

"Fuck, baby."

I hit my trigger when I heard the nickname, and I spiraled out of control when it hit me. I bit my bottom lip and screamed at the same time, relieved I could be as loud as I wanted. "God, Volt."

"Yes, I am your god." He gave a final thrust before he released inside me, giving me more seed than he ever had before. He deposited everything he had, like I was a bank account. "Shit, that felt good." He brushed his lips across my hairline before he looked me in the eye.

Volt was back. He returned to me, life coming back into his eyes. He stared at me like it was the first time he really looked at me. He rubbed his nose against mine before he kissed the corner of my mouth. "I love you."

Those words made me melt into a puddle. I was sticky and wet, mushy for him. "I love you too."

"I'm sorry I've been…not here."

"It's okay." I grazed my fingers against his cheek. "You're here now."

"Thanks for bringing me back to you."

"No problem. I know you'll always do the same for me."

***

Volt was never exactly who he used to be. But he was pretty close.

He took me out to dinner, made me laugh with his dirty jokes, and he gave me hot loving at night. Once in a while, his eyes would drift away in sadness, thinking about Clay and the last conversation they had. When that happened, I would say something to change the subject, something that made him laugh. Within minutes, he was back to normal.

The city was still frozen for winter, and the streets were caked with snow and frosty puddles. Steam erupted out of the sewer grates and spiraled high into the sky. People walked around with hot coffee in their hands, using the warm fuel to keep their legs moving.

Volt and I slowly returned to where we were before the breakup and the sad situation with Clay.

I was in the bar with Natalie as she talked about Jared. "He's really sweet. The other day, he sent me flowers at work—for no reason at all."

"Wow. Who knew he could be romantic?"

"And he's pretty good in bed too. No complaints."

"Thanks for the info but I never asked."

"Like you didn't tell me how good the sex was with Volt," she argued.

"Because you asked," I reminded her.

Natalie looked over my shoulder. "Here come the guys now. They see us, and Volt is checking out your ass so hard."

"Good. Wait until he sees the front of my dress." It was a sweetheart cut, and it showed my tits pressed tightly together. It wasn't the kind of dress I would wear if I were out on my own. I specifically wore it just for him.

"He'll be pleased to see the girls."

Volt reached my side, and the second he did, he wrapped his arm around me possessively, wanting there to be no mistake that I was his, and then he pulled me in for a kiss. His five o'clock shadow rubbed up against me, exciting me more than his lips did. "Hey."

"Hey." My legs already turned to jelly.

He looked down at my chest, noticing the special cut of the dress. His eyes were glued to my tits for nearly five seconds. "I like this..." He squeezed my waist.

"Why do you think I bought it?"

He pressed his lips to my ear. "So I would fuck you in the bathroom."

"It wouldn't be the worst thing in the world."

He wore his black blazer and dark jeans, his chest looking ripped in the gray shirt underneath. He started eating and hitting the gym again, transforming back into the strong man I loved having on top of me. "Watch what you wish for. It might come true."

"I'm down for some PDA."

"That's not PDA," he said with a chuckle. "That's straight up obscenity. And I like it."

Jared and Natalie were close together, whispering to each other as they shared kisses at the same time.

Derek arrived at our group, but he looked like he was about to throw up. "I need a girlfriend."

Volt turned to him. "You want my help?"

"I just want someone to make out with so I don't puke from watching all of you," Derek said.

"Like you won't beat off to this later," Volt teased.

"I beat off a lot," Derek said. "But never to you."

"Sure," Volt said. "Whatever you say."

"Julia told me she really hit it off with Sage," Derek said. "I guess they're getting serious."

"Wow," I said. "We're the perfect matchmakers."

"At least we repaired the damage we caused," Volt said. "We both wasted their time."

"Julia is definitely an upgrade for Sage, so he should be thanking me," I said.

Volt rolled his eyes. "Beauty is in the eye of the beholder. And you're the most beautiful woman I've ever met."

"Aww," I whispered.

Derek rolled his eyes. "I'm out of here." He walked away and headed to the bar.

"Poor guy," Jared said. "I think he's lonely."

"Know anyone to set him up with?" Volt asked.

"Nope," Jared said. "I don't have many girlfriends." He turned to Natalie. "Is there some single teacher you can hook him up with?"

"Ew," Natalie said. "I wouldn't recommend my brother to any of them. That would bite me in the ass later."

"He'll find someone, guys," I said. "Don't worry about him. Love will find him when it's ready to."

"Wise words, baby." Volt gave me a quick peck on the lips.

"So, let's get some drinks and start dancing." Natalie pulled Jared with her to the counter.

Volt didn't follow. He turned to me instead. "I feel like an old man."

"Why?"

"Because all I want to do is go home and be with you."

My heart melted at his words. I felt like a love struck teenager who couldn't control the butterflies in her stomach.

"I don't care for the bars, the music, or the people. I just want to go home and fuck you."

It wasn't sweet by any means, but I still loved hearing it. It was romantic to my ears, and it just made me want him more. "I'm down for the bathroom if you are."

"I thought you were classier than that."

"Not with you."

Chapter Nine

Volt

I thought about Clay every day, wondering how he was doing and if he was integrating with his new living situation. There were times when I wanted to call and check on him, but I knew he wouldn't take my calls. Taylor finally snapped me out of my depression, but that didn't mean I'd forgotten about him.

Continuing my lifeless existence hurt Taylor, and I couldn't afford to lose her again. So I cleaned up my act and finally started being there for her, living in the moment. Those hours when we were swept away in the throes of passion were the best.

Because I didn't think about anything else.

She became my drug, making me addicted to the way she made me feel. She pulled me through the darkness, taking me to the light on the other side of the tunnel. She took my hand and guided me forward, picking up the slack when I dropped it.

But then I checked the mail that afternoon.

Clay's SAT scores came in.

I forgot he had them sent to my house. He knew they would be safe there, kept in a place where his father wouldn't discover what kind of activities he'd been up to.

I sat at the kitchen table and stared at the envelope.

My first impulse was to rip it open and read it. I was eager to know how well he did. I knew he did amazing. That kid worked so hard to get these scores. I was too excited not to open it.

But I found the strength to set it down.

We needed to open it together.

Taylor came over after work, using her key to get inside. She stayed with me all the time now, her apartment forsaken. At that rate, she was basically paying for an expensive storage unit. "Hey."

"Hey, baby." I turned to her but didn't get up.

She walked over to me, wearing a black dress with a thick overcoat. "How was your day?"

I snatched her by the waist and pulled her into my lap. "My day is always terrible until I see you." I kissed her neck then the corner of her mouth.

Taylor shivered in my arms, pleased by the attention. "You're sweet."

I kissed her shoulder then handed over the letter. "Look what came in today."

She grabbed it and examined it. "Clay's test scores?"

I nodded.

"What are you going to do?"

"Go down there and hand it over. Hopefully, he'll open it with me."

"Yeah, that's a good idea."

"You think it's been long enough?"

"Yeah," she answered. "He's been there for a month. He's had time to adjust."

I wanted to see him—so much. I wanted to talk to him, take him out to do something fun. But I was afraid nothing had changed. He still hated me—loathed me. What if he refused to see me?

"Do you want me to come with you?"

"No," I answered. "I think it's best if it's just he and I."

"Okay." She rubbed my shoulder and kissed my forehead. "It'll be okay."

"I hope you're right."

"Underneath that anger and resentment is love. Don't forget that."

I nodded, holding on to those words.

***

After I signed in at the front, I was escorted to the back. It was an activities room, where TVs, toys, and games were placed. There were at least twenty kids there of all different ages.

My heart pumped hard in my chest. I could feel it thud against my ribs with every beat. I was sick to my stomach, nervous as hell. It was difficult to want something so bad but knowing you could never have it. I just wanted Clay back in my life. I wanted him to know I cared about him, that I would always look after him.

He was sitting by the window, his knees pulled to his chest. He wore the same baggy sweater he always wore. His hair was long because he hadn't had a haircut. He was isolated, ignoring the other kids and staring out the window in the hope of freedom.

He hated it here. I could tell.

I walked over to him with the letter tucked into my pocket. With every step closer, I felt more panicked. This would end in doom, but I had to try anyway. I took a seat beside him, waiting for him to notice me.

162

"What are you doing here?" His voice was quiet but it contained all his resentment.

"I wanted to see you." I wasn't happy to see that he was still as skinny as before. His clothes weren't any better, and his happiness seemed non-existent.

"Well, you see me. Now go."

I stayed in the same spot, refusing to budge. "I'm sorry you hate it here."

"Why should you be sorry?" he snapped. "You put me here."

"I hate to see that you're sad. But I'm glad you don't have any bruises or marks. I'd take that any day."

"A bruise will heal. But despair never does. It just lingers."

He never used to speak that way. His vocabulary had skyrocketed since we started working together. Every day, he showed me how much he learned without even realizing it. I was hurt by what he said, but extremely proud. "It's temporary. You'll be out of here in no time."

"No one is going to adopt me. Let's not kid ourselves."

"Even if they don't, you only have a year left."

163

"A year is torture. I can't go where I want when I want. I'm a bird stuck in a cage."

"Not being able to go where and when you want isn't a punishment. These people care about you and want you to be safe. That's all."

"They just want me to shut up and not bother them. They don't give a damn about me or any other kid in this place. They just take their check and go home. Don't sugarcoat this and make it into a fairytale. This place is a prison and we both know it."

Was he really that unhappy here? Or was he just being stubborn. "I'm sorry you feel that way."

"If you really cared about me, you would adopt me. You just threw me in here to ease your own conscious. You didn't do this for me. You did it for yourself." He looked out the window, his jaw clenched tightly. He stared at me as seldom as possible.

His words hit me like hot oil right out of the pan. They burned me everywhere, scarring me. Adopting him never crossed my mind. I didn't have the resources or the experience to raise a kid. I could help him part time, but not be a father. Shit, I could barely look after myself. I made stupid decisions left and right. When Sara broke my heart, I lost myself for a full year. "I would adopt you, but I can't give you what you need."

"Whatever," he said. "I don't even want you to adopt me. I'm just making a point."

Did he really mean that?

"Can you just go? There's nothing else to say, and I hate looking at you."

I kept telling myself he was only lashing out because he was hurt. He still cared about me. He didn't hate me like he claimed. He spent two weeks with me over Christmas break, and we had a great time. I didn't do that out of pity. I did it because I enjoyed spending time with him. "I brought something." I pulled out the letter. "Your SAT scores came in."

He flinched slightly, showing a different emotion besides hatred. But then he covered it up, pretending it never happened. "So what?"

"Let's open them."

"Doesn't matter anymore."

"Yes, it does. I know these scores are good. You worked your ass off for this. Let's celebrate together."

"I probably failed."

"You can't fail the SAT. I already explained that."

"Whatever," he said. "My score is probably bad."

"It's not." I held the letter out. "I know it's not."

He still wouldn't take it. "I'm not going to college, so what's the point?"

"You bet your ass you're going to college." My rule for no cussing was out the window. "Just because you're mad at me doesn't mean your future should be jeopardized. If you get a scholarship, you could go to school for free and get out of here within a year."

He pulled his legs closer to his chest but he didn't snap at me. I took that as a good sign.

"Come on." I held the letter out to him.

He eyed it for a while without taking it.

"I'm not opening it for you."

He finally snatched it and stared at the letter. He didn't open it, just looked at his name on the envelope. He finally ripped the top off and pulled out the paper. Instead of reading it, he just held it.

"Don't be afraid. There's nothing in that letter that can hurt you."

Clay still wouldn't read it. "What if it's bad?"

"It's not."

"But what if it is?" he demanded. "What will I do then?"

"Hypothetically, if these scores are bad, it's not the end of the world."

"But I won't go to college. I won't get a good job."

"Not true. You don't need the SAT for a junior college. Go there for two years then transfer. They'll take you if you have good grades."

"But I want to go to a four year..." He folded the paper in his hands, unable to look at it. This whole time, he pretended nothing good would happen in his life, but he'd secretly been hoping for the best.

"I know those scores are good, Clay."

"No, you don't. Neither one of us do."

"I tutored you every single day for eight months. You were a different person when we started, and you soared beyond my every expectation. You're a very smart kid. I don't think you understand what you're capable of."

He took a breath before he unfolded the letter. He browsed through the introduction before he flipped the page over. At the bottom were the two scores separately and the score combined.

I held my breath and waited.

Clay didn't react. He just stared.

"Clay?" I pressed.

"Uh…"

"What is it?"

"I don't know. I'm not sure how to read it."

"Can I see it?" I extended my hand.

He handed it over. "It says I got a 500. Which means…I'm stupid."

"Not possible. You read it wrong." I grabbed the paper and looked at the bottom. In bold letters were the two separate numbers. He got a 600 for the verbal portion and a 500 on the math portion. Combined, he got an 1100.

Holy shit.

"I screwed it up. I was nervous and there were so many people there—"

"Clay, this is outstanding." I stood up, unable to sit still for a moment longer. "This is…amazing. This is incredible. I can't believe it."

"A 500?" he asked incredulously.

"That's your math score," I explained. "Combined, you got an 1100. Clay, that's huge. You can go to a state school, no problem."

"Really?" He finally let his hatred go. "Are you lying?"

"No. Man, I'm so proud of you. You worked so hard for this. Every day..." I felt the paper in my hands, feeling like I finally did something worthwhile in my life. Clay did all the work, but I helped him get there. And the finish line was bittersweet. "This is so great."

He took the paper back and stared at it, looking at the combined score.

I ran my hand through my hair, smiling for the first time since I got there. "You're awesome, you know that? That was all you."

He kept the paper and folded it up, tucking it into his back pocket. "Well, at least I'm not as dumb as I thought."

"You were never dumb."

"I guess I'll apply for schools now..."

"We can do that together. I'll walk you through it."

"Why would I want your help?" he asked viciously.

My happiness evaporated quicker than water in the desert.

"Thanks for helping me with the SAT and everything, but that doesn't change anything. You still stabbed me in the back."

"Clay, come on."

"No. You betrayed me. I don't want anything to do with you." The hurt shined in his eyes when he looked at me. "I'm not trying to sounds like a punk, but we did what we set out to do. There's no reason for us to keep talking. You made your choice when you threw me under the bus. Now, go."

"Clay, I care about you. I think I proved it with those SAT scores."

"And you proved otherwise when you ratted me out. I'm in a prison because of you."

"I'm sorry, okay? I was trying to protect you."

"Well, you didn't. You just made my life more difficult. I don't have a lot of people I can rely on. At first, I didn't trust you, but then you proved yourself to me. I thought I finally had someone in my life...like how people have family and friends. But then all that went to shit. You're just like everyone else. I shouldn't have trusted you, and I'll never make that mistake again." He looked out the window, shutting me out.

"Clay—"

"Go. If you don't, I'll scream and they'll throw you out."

How did our relationship turn to this? "I know one day you'll understand what I did and why I did it. And when that day comes, no matter how far into the future, you know where to find me."

"So I can apologize?" he asked incredulously.

"No. So we can be friends again."

***

Taylor was there when I walked inside. "How'd it go?"

With heavy feet, I entered the apartment and threw my jacket on the chair. It slid to the floor, but I didn't care enough to pick it up.

Taylor got her answer just by looking at me. She recognized the despair in my eyes and knew my afternoon with Clay had taken a turn for the worst. Now, she looked at a hollow man, broken and defeated. "I'm sorry..."

Instead of shutting her out like I did last time, I used her as a crutch. I wrapped my arms around her and used her as much as possible. Her love kept me balanced, and the sadness in her eyes made me feel less alone. We were in this together. She carried half the weight with me, making the burden less painful. "I know."

"How were his scores?"

That was the one thing that gave me joy. "Amazing."

"Aww...that's so great."

"An 1100. Can you believe it?"

"Wow." She pulled away so she could look at my face. "Are you serious?"

I nodded, unable to wipe the pride off my face. Clay worked his ass off for that, and I was proud of him. He worked against the odds and started at a lower level than most kids, but he quickly passed them with determination and hard work. "Yeah. But I wasn't surprised."

"Go, Clay."

"We studied for eight months for that exam. He paid his dues."

"That means he can go to a great college."

"Yeah. A lot of them will ignore his grades because his score shows he clearly knows the material."

"I'm so happy to hear that."

"Me too. He deserves it."

"So, are you going to help him with the college application process?"

That's where things went to shit. "He doesn't want my help."

"Oh..."

"He told me to get out and never come back."

"He's just upset right now. He'll come around."

"No, he won't." There was a difference between being stubborn and being hurt. He was too hurt to forgive me. There was no other way around it. "He said it would be different if I adopted him, but he knows that's never going to happen."

"Well, that would be ludicrous. You can't adopt anyone."

"I know." Being responsible for a whole other person was something I couldn't handle. I was far too childish and selfish to take care of someone else. Taylor was my second girlfriend in my entire life. Did I really have enough life experience to take care of another human being? Doubtful.

"Someone will adopt him."

"No, they won't." I wouldn't lie about that part. "No one wants a rough high school kid. He's going to be eighteen soon anyway. Not much point."

"I guess..."

"But he'll only be there for another year, and then he'll be gone. It can't be worse than living with his father, but he says otherwise."

She rubbed my shoulders, powerless to do anything else to chase away this pain. "I'm sorry about all of this. You sacrificed so much for him. You did more than anyone else. And he doesn't appreciate it."

"I don't care if he appreciates it. I just don't want him to hate me."

"One day he'll realize it. I know he will."

I wasn't betting on it.

"But you can't let this drag you down. You've given him enough. Don't give him your happiness too."

"I know…" I couldn't do that to Taylor again. I became the world's worst boyfriend for two weeks straight. I was a living zombie around the house, not listening to anything she said. I hardly looked at her most of the time. "Don't worry. I won't break down like that again."

She cupped my face and gave me a soft kiss. "I know. But if you do, you know I'm right here next to you."

***

I walked into her classroom after the bell rang. The kids filed out, pushing past me in a hurry. It was snowing outside and my overcoat was caked with patches of white snow on the shoulders. I wiped them away before I approached her desk.

She looked cute sitting there, wearing a long sleeve red dress with her hair in pretty curls. She was going over papers while sitting on her desk, her lips pressed tightly together as she tried to finish everything as quickly as possible, in a hurry to get home to me.

"Hey, baby."

She looked up at the sound of my voice, and her mouth immediately melted into a smile. "What a nice surprise."

I leaned over the table and gave her a PG kiss.

"What are you doing here?"

"I had a meeting with my dad about the SAT scores. The kids did well. He was impressed."

"He shouldn't be impressed. You're amazing at what you do."

"Why, thank you." I leaned over again and gave her another kiss. "That deserves another kiss."

Now her eyes smiled just as much as her lips. "You look really handsome today."

"Oh no," I said with a chuckle. "We're on a bad road now."

She grabbed my tie and wrapped it around her fingers, keeping me stationed over her. "How about I lock the door and we take our chances?"

"Sex in a classroom?" Doing something so illegal got me hard in my slacks. Forbidden and taboo things were my forte. But it was a serious crime since minors were around. If we got caught, there would be talk of jail time. "As enticing as that sounds, we shouldn't."

"Where's my fearless man?"

"I'll fuck you in an alley behind a dumpster. How about that?"

She chuckled. "Too dirty for me. And you know how dirty I am…"

"Then we'll have to settle for some old-fashioned vanilla sex in our apartment." I constantly referred to my place as our place. She was there all the time anyway, only going home to get more supplies. We lived together without officially living together.

Maybe we should make it official.

Instead of freaking me out, the idea actually pleased me. If she moved all her stuff over, then she would never have a reason to leave. She would always be right beside me.

And that sounded like heaven.

"What are you thinking?" She still held my tie in her fingers.

I held her gaze, my eyes concentrating on the deep blue of her eyes. Maybe I should invite her to move in with me right then and there. It was a big step, considering we hadn't been formally dating very long, a few months tops. But this felt right. It felt right from the beginning, from the day I saw her on the sidewalk with a map of New York in her hands. "Move in with me." It wasn't a question because I wouldn't accept any other answer than the one I wanted. I was telling her what to do, refusing to give her any options.

Her fingers immediately slackened around my tie, and her playful eyes turned to shock. That was the last thing she expected me to say. It took her a few seconds to recover from the bomb I dropped, and when she did, happiness slowly emerged. "You're serious?"

"Do I look anything but serious?" Both of my hands were on the desk, leaning over her the same way I did when we were in bed together. "I want you there every day. I hate it when you leave. So how about you just stop leaving?"

"It's a big step..."

"Not really." The fact I came up with the idea at all told me it wasn't a big deal. It was something that would truly make me happy. She was my best friend, and even when I wasn't taking her on my bed, I still wanted to be around her. I wanted to play video games with her, make dinner with her, and watch her favorite movies even though I thought they were annoying. Would anything change in a year? In two years?

"So, you're sure you want this?"

"Goddammit, just say yes."

She grinned. "I thought you weren't asking me?"

Shit, she caught me there.

She placed her face against mine. "Yes."

Happiness washed through me, and I felt like the luckiest guy in the world. After almost losing her, I realized how empty my life would have been. The more of Taylor I had, the better off I was. This was the right decision for both of us. "That was the right answer."

Just before I kissed her, the door flew open. The guy I saw kissing her a while ago walked inside. He held a beaker in his hand and seemed to be returning it.

My nostrils flared like a bull and I stood upright, ready to charge this guy down and rip his insides out. He touched my girl without permission, pressed his nerdy lips against her mouth, and I wasn't cool with that.

He flinched when he saw me, almost dropping the beaker. He put two and two together, and knew he was dead meat.

Taylor grabbed my wrist. "Volt." She didn't want me to maul her colleague.

But he should have thought of that before he kissed my lady.

He turned to the door and quickly ran out like a chicken shit. He almost dropped the beaker again on his way out, and when he was in the hallway, the sound of shattering glass was heard.

"Fucking piece of shit."

"Volt, calm down."

I eyed the door, hoping he would come back.

"He didn't know I had a boyfriend. When I told him, he felt bad."

"That doesn't mean you can just kiss someone."

"You did it to me," she argued.

"That's different."

"How so?" she countered.

"Because you were mine. You've always been mine."
My words didn't match my facial expression at all. I was
still livid, and a little insane. "Maybe you should transfer to
another school."

"Please don't tell me you're threatened by him. He
really is harmless."

"Whatever you say."

"After that afternoon, he's been nothing but
professional. I can tell it was an honest mistake."

"He's still a fucking asshole."

She came around the desk and wrapped her arms
around my neck, blocking my view of the door. "So, am I
going to get my own dresser? Am I going to have half the
closet or the whole thing?" She changed the course of my
thoughts by mentioning something that made me happy.

My nostrils stopped flaring. "You can have your own
dresser."

"Perfect. What about the closet?"

"You can have the closet in the spare bedroom."

"Excellent." She leaned in and gave me a slow kiss,
slowly massaging my mouth and giving me a little tongue.

When she did that, all other thoughts ceased. I
wanted to bend her over the desk and take her right then

and there. I didn't care about getting caught. I didn't care about the police.

I just cared about her.

***

"This is weird." Derek stared at me from across the table, a beer sitting in front of him.

"What's weird?" We were in a booth near the window. People passed on the sidewalk, huddled tightly in their thick clothing. It would be cold for a few months until spring saved us. Personally, I'd take the freezing cold over a hot summer day in New York. The humidity was a bitch.

"That it's just you and me. You're always with Taylor."

"Are you saying I don't spend enough time with you?"

"No. But maybe I'm lonely. Jared is busy with my sister now. I'm on my own."

"So, this is a pity party for yourself?" I asked incredulously.

"It just sucks when my two best friends are tied down. No one wants to go out anymore. They just want to stay home and paint their nails and shit."

"Okay, I've never done that before."

"Wait for it." He held up a hand. "Jared told me it happened to him. Haven't been able to look at him the same."

I chuckled. "I may be a pussy, but I'm not that big of a pussy."

"We'll see."

I didn't realize how much I was neglecting my friend. I really did spend all my time with Taylor. I didn't even notice. "Want to watch the game tomorrow at that pizza place?"

"Hell yeah," he said excitedly. "No girlfriend, right?"

"No girlfriend."

"Sweet." He finally drank his beer, in a better mood.

"Sorry I've neglected you. I always told myself I wouldn't be that friend. But obviously, it happened anyway."

"Nah, it's alright," he said. "It happens. People grow up and move on with their lives. I'm just a little late."

"You'll find the right person. Just keep your eyes peeled."

He shrugged.

"So…I asked Taylor to move in with me."

"You did?" he asked in surprise. "Wow. Took you long enough."

"What?" I asked with a laugh. "I thought you would say it's too soon."

"Not really. You've been together for over a year now."

"Not officially."

"You didn't have a label but whatever. You were in love with each other so it counts."

"I guess."

"I'm glad you guys figured out your problems. I was worried for a minute."

He was the one who suggested coming clean about Sara. And it ended up saving my relationship. "I told her what happened with Sara."

His eyes didn't blink as he stared at me, waiting for the explanation he so desperately craved. He asked me about it a million times over the years, but I never answered. Now I didn't see the point in hiding it. "You remember the night I called you and said I got the ring?"

He nodded, too nervous to speak.

"And we were going to meet at Tito's?"

"Yeah."

"Well, I got there first. And when I walked inside, I saw her making out with her ex."

"Holy shit."

"They were going at it like animals. It was clear it wasn't just an innocent run in. She'd been screwing him for a while."

He ran his fingers through his hair, distressed. "Fuck. What did you do?"

"Nothing."

"Nothing?" he asked.

"I turned around and walked out. I gave the ring to a bum on the sidewalk and told him to pawn it for cash."

"Are you insane? Wasn't that ring ridiculously expensive?"

"Yeah. But I would never want the money I spent on her. It was tainted. I'd rather give it away than let that cash sit in my bank account."

"What a whore. What happened then?"

"I broke up with her."

"What did you say?"

"That I didn't want to be with her anymore. I didn't really give an explanation. She kept asking what was wrong, and I kept saying I just didn't care anymore. She didn't do anything for me."

"Burn..."

"I knew not telling her the truth would haunt her forever. She would never know why I left. She would never know what went wrong. She would grow paranoid and wonder if she'd been caught but she couldn't ask me for fear of giving herself away. I thought that was a better punishment than confronting her."

Derek hung on to my every word. "I guess. Never thought about it."

"She kept calling me after we broke up, but I never took her calls. I went from being hopelessly in love with her to not giving a damn. That had to hurt."

"Vicious."

I shrugged, not feeling bad about it.

"Why didn't you tell me before?"

"I was embarrassed. I called and said I got the ring...and then I found out she was sneaking around behind my back. I just felt stupid. Just ten minutes before that, I was buying a huge engagement ring, not having a clue she was sucking someone else's dick."

"That's not embarrassing," Derek argued. "You were the victim."

"But I shouldn't have let myself be the victim. That means I wasn't enough for her. And not being enough for someone is humiliating."

Derek shook his head. "That thought never would have crossed my mind—or anyone else's. You're being way too hard on yourself."

"I wouldn't say that. It was just embarrassing. I told my parents I was going to propose, and they were all excited. And then I had to tell them what happened and break their hearts. If I never told them about the ring, I could have just said Sara and I broke up. But since they knew how serious it was, I couldn't make up a lie that would make sense. The whole thing just sucked."

"Yeah, I get it. But I still don't know why you couldn't tell me."

"It was nothing personal, man. I was just...it was too hard for me. As much as I hate to admit it, she really fucked me up. I was so heartbroken...I couldn't think straight."

He nodded, sympathizing with me. "Now I understand why you behaved the way you did. One moment you were in a relationship, and then the next moment, you were screwing everyone in the city."

"I just snapped."

"Yeah. I get it."

"And then Taylor came out of nowhere and...fixed me." It was a cheesy thing to say.

But Derek didn't make fun of me. "She's a good catch. You could do a lot worse."

"I know. She's perfect." I looked down at my whiskey, thinking of her eyes as they stared into mine when we were making love.

"I think Taylor is the real deal. You aren't going to have the same experience as you did with Sara."

"I know." I wasn't worried about it. I loved Sara but she was never my best friend, not like Taylor was. When I looked back on our relationship, I wasn't sure why I was so fascinated with her. She really didn't have a lot to offer other than her looks. Taylor was a bombshell and the biggest sweetheart in the world. She was way out of my league and always would be. "That's why I asked her to move in with me."

"Girl roommate." He winked. "Nice."

I chuckled. "I like walking in on her when she's in the shower. Because, you know, tits."

He laughed. "Tits are nice." He clanked his glass against mine. "I'm happy for you."

"Thanks."

"I'm going to be the best man at your wedding, right?"

"Absolutely," I said with a smile.

"I'm surprised you didn't just ask her to marry you."

The thought crossed my mind. It came up more often than I expected it to. Our relationship had progressed until it reached the sky. It didn't seem like it could get any better. We were happy together, madly in love. Was there anything else to wait for? "I thought about it."

"Why didn't you go for it?"

"I don't know. Do you think she'd say yes?"

He rolled his eyes. "She would have said yes the day you met."

I took a drink of my whiskey to cover my thoughts.

"Dude, when you know, you just know."

"What's that supposed to mean?"

"You know you found the right person. I'm not trying to push you into something you aren't ready for, but we both know this is going to last forever. We both know she's your wife somewhere down the road. Why not now? Why later?"

My eyes narrowed. "When did you become a hopeless romantic?"

"I'm not," he snapped. "But if I were in your situation, I know I wouldn't wait. It's obvious you guys are meant to be together. Okay...maybe that does make me sound like a romantic."

"And a pussy."

"But it's true. You just know it's going to last forever."

The thought gave me a temporary high before I came crashing down. "I thought the same thing with Sara..."

"That was different, man."

"How so?"

"You guys didn't click the way you and Taylor do. She was your first relationship so you didn't know any better. You cared more about the way Sara looked than her boring personality. But with Taylor, you know she has the full package."

She did have the full package.

"Now you know, for sure, who you should be with."

There was never a doubt that Taylor was the woman I was supposed to be with. I wanted her for the rest of my life. She would be honest and faithful. She would give me children and grow old with me, still laughing even when our bones and joints ached. She would make me so happy I would forget what it was like to be miserable.

He held up his hands. "Do what you want. I'm not pushing you in any specific direction. But don't let your experience with Sara affect your decisions with Taylor. Because if that bullshit never happened, I know you would be proposing right now."

I stared at the ice cubes in my glass and stirred them around with a jolt of my wrist. I knew he was right. I was letting the past affect my future—even now. I wasn't afraid of commitment, but I was afraid of being reminded how shitty that evening felt when I spotted Sara with someone else.

Derek stared at me quietly, waiting for me to say something.

I kept thinking to myself, wondering what to do next.

"Earth to Volt." He waved a hand in front of my face.

I looked up from my glass. "I'm going to ask her to marry me."

He grinned from ear-to-ear, the kind of smile that reached his eyes and every other part of his body. "Fuck yeah. That's what I'm talking about. And I'm your best man. Jared can be a loser groomsman."

"Let's not rush the wedding. I still have to ask."

"She'll say yes, and we both know it. Now let's go get that ring." He rubbed his palms together.

"Why are you so excited about this?" I asked. "Guys don't care about this stuff."

"You're my best friend. And I want you to be happy. She makes you happy, ergo, you should marry her."

It was a sweet thing to say, something more affectionate than he would normally say. "Well, thanks. You've always been a good friend to me, even when I wasn't the best to you."

"Oh, shut up," he said. "Now we just sound like a bunch of girls."

I laughed. "We really do."

He slid out of the booth and left the cash on the table. "Now let's go shopping."

I rolled my eyes.

Chapter Ten

Taylor

"So what does Volt do?" Sara walked beside me, holding a Gucci bag that contained a new sweater inside.

"He owns his own company."

"So, he must make bank?"

"Uh…I guess." I never asked Volt about his finances. I knew he was wealthy because of his penthouse overlooking Central Park and the Maserati parked in his garage, not to mention his expensive suits and other knick-knacks.

"Like, how much are we talking?"

What did it matter? "I don't know. I've never asked."

"Really?" she asked in surprise. "This is important information if you're going to marry him."

"Well, rich or poor, it doesn't matter to me."

Sara had always cared about security and having nice things.

"By the way, he asked me to move in with him."

"Seriously?" She stopped walking and stared at me.

"Yep." I already packed most of my things in boxes and prepared for the move. I just had to figure out what to do with my old furniture. There was no place for it in his apartment.

"Wow. That's great."

"I know. I'm excited."

"I can't believe you're going to be living with this guy but I haven't met him."

I know. Every time we arranged something, it fell through. "You want to meet him now? He should be home."

"Yeah, of course."

We walked a few blocks before we reached the building. She looked up and admired the view. "Wow. Definitely loaded."

I rolled my eyes.

"And you're moving in here?"

"Well, my apartment is way too small." We took the elevator to the top floor then walked inside. "Volt, I'm here. And Sara is with me."

Sara shut the door behind her and took a look around his luxurious place. "He's super loaded."

"Shh!" I didn't want Volt to hear that.

"You made the right choice moving in here. It's so nice."

"Volt?" I set my purse down and came farther into the room. "Are you here?"

There was no response.

"Hmm." I wasn't sure where he would be. I pulled out my phone and texted him. *Hey, I just got home. Where are you?*

Hey, baby. I'm hanging out with Derek. Sorry, I forgot to let you know.

It's okay. When will you be home?

We're going to grab dinner and watch the game. I probably won't be home until bedtime.

Okay. I tried not to be disappointed. I didn't mind him going out with Derek. I just missed him. *I'll see you then.*

You better be awake when I get there—and naked.

I smiled. *Will do.*

Love you.

I melted when I saw those words. *Love you too.* I set down my phone and turned back to Sara. "I guess he's out for the night."

"Oh, really?" she asked in disappointment. "I need to meet this incredible man. The suspense is killing me."

"It's killing me too."

"Well, you want to get dinner since you're free?"

"Sure. Let's get a drink too."

"Now you're thinking."

By the time Volt came home, I was already in bed. I tried to stay naked, but it was too cold. I ended up putting on his t-shirt and sweatpants. I read off my phone in bed until I heard the front door open and shut.

He came down the hall a moment later, still wearing the suit he wore to work.

"Long day?"

He removed his tie, his eyes trained on me. "Why aren't you naked?"

"I was cold." I set my phone aside and sat up.

He tore off each article of clothing, stripping down until he was completely naked. His cock was hard and throbbing, eager for some rough sex.

Now I wasn't cold at all.

He climbed over the bed and dragged me by the ankle until I was underneath him. He stripped me down harshly, getting my clothes off as quickly as possible. Thirst was in his eyes, and he was desperate to drink me.

When I was naked, he wrapped my legs around his waist and shoved himself inside me, stretching me with no warning whatsoever. His hand moved to the back of my hair and he yanked it, keeping my chin up and my eyes on him.

I liked it.

He thrust into me hard, taking me like he owned me and was the commander of every part of me. He moaned from deep in his chest when he felt the moisture between my legs and he rammed into me harder.

I was already going to come.

"I missed you." He breathed hard on top of me, breaking a sweat from the exertion.

"I missed you too." My nails dug into him harshly, on the verge of drawing blood. I loved the sweet and sensual lovemaking we did, but I loved this even more. I loved the way he pushed me down into submission, taking me because I was his.

He continued to thrust inside me, his cock becoming harder as he approached his climax. I could feel it thicken, desperate to release inside me. He dug his pelvic bone into me harder, rubbing against my clit so I would explode.

After three more thrusts, I was there. "Right there..." My head rolled back as I felt the power slam into me.

He fisted my hair and yanked my head until I was facing him again. "Look at me when you come."

My orgasm was that much harder, hotter. I gripped his arms as I held on, feeling my body tighten as the pleasure took me sky-high. I saw the dark desire in his eyes. He was loving the face I made when I crumbled for him.

A grunt escaped his throat, and he released deep inside me, giving me all of his seed until there was nothing left to give. He shoved himself as far as he could go, hitting my cervix as he released. "Baby…"

We finished our high together, falling into the mutual passion we had for each other. Somehow, that orgasm was even better than all the rest. He made my toes curl and my breath hitch. He sent me into the clouds, high above the ground until I reached the heavens. "You always make me come so hard."

He kept his dick inside me, having no intention of pulling it out anytime soon. "And it's always a pleasure." He scooted me up the bed and laid me down, snuggling with me under the covers. He didn't pull his cock out because he planned to take me again the second he was at full length.

"Did you and Derek have fun?"

"Yeah. But not as much fun as we just had." He kissed my neck then my nose.

"Sara came over for a little while. She was hoping to meet you but you weren't home."

"That's ironic. I'm always home."

"I know."

"Arrange a dinner. I'll finally meet this amazing best friend of yours."

"Alright, I will. How about this weekend?"

"Sounds like a date."

"Perfect."

"Did you tell her you're moving in with me?"

"Yep."

"Was she supportive?"

"Yeah. When she saw your place, she almost had a heart attack."

"Why?" he asked. "What's wrong with it?"

"She thinks you're loaded."

He kept a straight face as he spoke. "I am loaded."

"But she seemed surprised by it."

"I own a company that has expanded into several different cities. I help people and make money at the same time. It's a nice set-up."

"Well, I think she's jealous."

"A lot of people are."

"I had to remind her I wasn't with you for your money. She kinda cares about those sorts of things."

"All women do."

"No, that's not true." I certainly didn't.

"Admit it. The fact I'm wealthy makes me more attractive."

"I really don't care." I'd never been a gold digger. All I cared about was a man who pulled his own weight. Someone who was passionate about his work. But that was it.

"Really?" he asked. "So if I were delivering pizzas, you'd be snuggled up with me right now."

"Well...delivering pizzas would make you a completely different person. So, probably not. But if you were a teacher that didn't make much, I wouldn't care. I'd like the fact you helped kids as your passion."

"Maybe I deliver pizza because it's my passion."

"Then you aren't passionate about the things I care about." It was a stupid conversation. I wasn't even sure why we were having it. "Let's change the subject."

"No. It's interesting."

"How?"

"I just think money has more to do with a relationship than you realize."

"Again, I don't feel that way."

"But I do." He squeezed my hip with his hand. "I like knowing I can take care of you. I like knowing you could quit your job whenever you felt like it and raise our kids. I like knowing I can buy you whatever the hell you want without breaking the bank. Money means something to me."

When he put it like that, it was sweet.

"Every woman wants to be taken care of. You aren't any different. And you know what? That's perfectly fine. Because if I couldn't take care of you, then I wouldn't be good enough for you."

"But I can take care of myself."

"One day you won't be able to. And I'll be there." He rubbed his nose against mine. "I want to give you half of what's mine. I want to give you my name. I want to give you everything—my empire." He looked me in the eye, showing me his sincerity.

Our relationship fell to a deeper level. I wanted to marry him but I never told him that. He never told me either. But now we were confessing how we really felt. Now that I was moving in with him, I realized exactly what our future held. One day, we would get married. One day, we would have a family.

It was actually happening.

And that made me happier than I could understand. It brought tears to my eyes, and I couldn't control them. They bubbled from my eyes and fell into the corners.

Volt watched them, understanding what the emotion meant. He pressed his lips to the corners of my eyes and kissed the tears away. "I love you too."

Chapter Eleven

Volt

The second Mom opened the door, she peered around for Taylor, expecting her to be right by my side. When she wasn't there, Mom looked at me in pure disappointment, as if she didn't want to see me unless Taylor was there too. "Taylor isn't coming?"

I told her I had plans with Derek. I needed to speak to my parents alone, preparing them for what was about to come. "She couldn't make it. You know, she has to prepare for class tomorrow."

"She's such a hard worker." Mom gave me a half-assed hug then led me inside. "We're having lasagna for dinner. Hope you're hungry."

I was always hungry for my mom's cooking. "Starving." I took off my heavy coat and greeted Dad. He was drinking whiskey so I poured myself a glass. My love for hard liquor started when I was sixteen, when my father and I used to drink together in the den.

We sat down at the table and talked about work and the winter chill outside. They asked about Clay, and I brushed over the fight he and I had. I didn't want to get into it. It would just bum me out, and it would make my parents sad too. "Actually, there's something I want to talk about." It felt oddly similar to last time. I went over there and told them I was going to ask Sara to marry me. They were thrilled, on the verge of tears. Connor even seemed slightly excited about it. Everything felt the same—except he wasn't there.

"What is it, baby?" Mom asked.

I didn't have any doubts about what I was going to do. I just hoped they would take me seriously. I already claimed I would love one person forever and that went to shit. Maybe it would explode in my face all over again. "I asked Taylor to move in with me."

"You did?" Mom asked. "Why would you do that?" She was still traditional even though the rest of the United States wasn't.

"Good for you," Dad said. "It's always good to live with someone before deciding if you want to marry them."

"Well…that's the thing." I stared at their faces before I continued. "I do want to marry her. And I'm going to propose." I reached into my inside jacket pocket and pulled out the black box. I set it in the center of the table where they could see it.

Mom covered her mouth but didn't gasp.

Dad stared at it, shocked.

"I asked her to move in with me because I thought it would be easier. I've already been down this road once before, and I didn't want to go there again. But then I realized I was being stupid. So, I'm going to ask her."

Mom was still in shock.

Dad was the first one to go for the ring. He opened the box and revealed a beautiful solitary diamond. It was nothing like the ring I bought for Sara. This one was simple and beautiful—just like Taylor. And it was twice as expensive. It would sparkle with brightness, keeping away any lookers. It was the clearest and most obvious way to tell the world she was mine—and to keep their hands off.

Mom finally reacted after several breaths. "Volt...it's so beautiful."

"I think she'll like it."

She took it from my father and examined it with a woman's eyes. "My god, this is gorgeous. She'll love it."

"I think so too."

Tears came into her eyes, right on cue. "Volt, this makes me so happy. We were worried you would never give love another chance. We thought that whore broke your spirit."

"Let's not talk about her." She was a thing of the past, not worth mentioning.

"You're right," Mom said. "Your father and I would love to have Taylor as a part of this family."

"I know." I knew they loved Taylor and would be happy about this.

"When are you going to ask her?" Dad asked.

"When she moves in with me. I'll have one extra box left over, and when she opens it, the ring will be inside. And then I'll get down on one knee."

"Aww..." Mom fanned her eyes. "That's so romantic."

"I don't think she'll expect it. It doesn't make sense for me to ask her to move in and then propose immediately afterward. It's the perfect plan."

"I like it," Dad said. "She'll never forget it."

I took the ring back and placed it in my pocket. "I just wanted to give you a heads-up."

"We appreciate it," Mom said. "We're so excited. I'm not sure if I can wait that long."

"Well, you're going to have to keep your lips sealed," I said. "Especially you, Dad."

Dad rolled his eyes. "You don't need to worry about me."

"Okay."

"Did you ask her parents?" Mom asked.

"I got their number from her phone when she was asleep and called them."

"Oh, good," Mom said. "What did they say?"

"They're really excited," I explained. "But not excited that she'll be living in New York for the rest of her life."

"Maybe they'll move here," Mom suggested.

"Maybe," I said with a shrug.

"Well, you did a good job with that ring," Dad said. "You don't need to buy her anything else expensive for a very long time."

"Good to know," I said with a chuckle.

"I'll call your brother after dinner. He'll be excited too."

I doubted he would care. "Good idea." I was finished with dinner and didn't want any pie so I excused myself. "Well, I should get going. I've got a lot of stuff to think about for the next week."

Both of my parents hugged me, happier than ever. They weren't just happy with the woman I chose to settle down with. They were happy I recovered from that horrific nightmare that Sara caused. They were relieved I found myself again—found joy.

***

"You're free Friday night?" Taylor asked from the couch. She was sitting in front of the TV with her schoolwork surrounding her. The TV was on and her favorite reality showed played.

"How are you supposed to get stuff done when you're so distracted?"

"It really slows me down," she said. "But I never have time to do normal stuff so I try to do both."

"You do normal stuff." I stripped off my coat and hung it by the door. "You roll around with me every night."

"Yeah, that's not normal. Every woman wishes she were doing that."

I waggled my eyebrows. "Thanks for the compliment."

"Are you going to answer my question or what?"

"What was the question? If I want to roll around with you right now? I'm game."

She rolled her eyes. "We're having dinner with Sara on Friday. You were supposed to meet her twice, and it never happened. Are you going to meet her this time?"

"Yes, baby. Just chill."

"Alright. She's starting to think I'm hiding you from her."

"Because you're afraid she won't keep her hands off me?" I winked and sat beside her on the couch.

She rolled her eyes again. "Yes. That's it."

"Don't worry. I'll make sure she keeps her hands to herself."

"I just want her to know I'm not embarrassed of you. That you aren't grotesquely disfigured."

"Wow...this took a bad turn."

She laughed and set her mound of papers aside. "She's been my best friend since we were two. That's a long time."

"Longer than I've known Derek."

"So, I want this to go well. If we're going to be together, I want her to be on board. I want the three of us to be able to hang out. And when she finds someone, I want us to double date."

It sounded boring to me, but I would give her whatever she wanted. I patted her thigh. "Baby, it'll be fine. I'll dazzle her."

"I know you will."

"So, did you finish moving all your stuff?" The living room was empty but the bedrooms had boxes littered everywhere. For one woman in a tiny apartment, she came with a lot of shit.

"Not quite. I still have a few more things to organize and pack up."

"Really drawing it out, huh?"

"I have two months left on my lease anyway, so I'm not in a hurry to clean up shop."

"You should be in a hurry to live with a sexy stud like me." I squeezed her thigh.

She eyed me carefully, like she saw something I didn't mean to show. "Why are you in such a good mood lately?"

"What?" I blurted. "I'm not."

"Yeah. You've been skipping around like the first day of spring has just arrived."

Was I making it that obvious? What if she figured out my plan? What if I ruined everything? "I'm just trying to be more positive. The whole thing with Clay really got me down, but I'm trying to be more uplifting."

She accepted the claim without hesitation. "Well, I'm glad to hear that."

Phew. Crisis averted. "So…are you done grading?"

"Why?"

I nodded toward the bedroom. "I'm craving an innocent schoolteacher at the moment." If she looked at my slacks, she would've seen my hard-on. It was easily distinguishable.

"Who said anything about innocent?"

"Ooh…a naughty schoolteacher. Even better."

She left the couch and pulled me behind her. "I'm craving an executive—medium well."

I watched her ass sway as I walked behind her. "I like my meat well done."

***

I wore a gray V-neck under my black blazer along with my dark jeans. Taylor didn't tell me what to wear, but I knew what she liked and didn't like. She preferred my laid-back clothes, not the stiff suits I wore to work every day. But she liked my blazer because it outlined my sculpted shoulders.

I knew what my lady liked.

She wore a tight black dress that hugged her petite waist and framed her boobalicious chest.

Sometimes, I didn't know what I liked more. Her ass in my face when I took her from behind, or those off-the-hook tits. Maybe I would never know. Maybe it was a tie. "You look smokin'."

She set her phone in her clutch and closed it. "Thanks. You look handsome too."

"Handsome enough for a quickie?"

"Nope. We're already running late." She pulled a black jacket over her body, hiding her gorgeous figure. She pulled her hair out from underneath the coat and adjusted it around her face.

"If we're already running late, why not?"

She rolled her eyes. "You're out of control."

"Out of control for you." I waggled my eyebrows.

She didn't bother responding and headed to the door. "We'll have sex behind a dumpster on the way home."

"Or how about in the bathroom stall? Even better."

"I'll think about it."

"Or how about—"

"I'll let you tit-fuck me when we get home if you behave."

That was an excellent bargaining chip, and she had me. Tit-fucking her was the best. She had the nicest tits ever. "You got it, baby."

***

Taylor looked at her phone before we entered the restaurant. "She said she's already here. She has a table in the back."

I opened the door for her then walked in behind her. "Good. That means there will be a basket of bread. And if this girl knows what she's doing, there will be a bottle of wine too."

Taylor took my hand and walked with me. "Just be yourself."

"I can't completely be myself. Otherwise, all I would do is tell her how nice your tits are. The night could get uncomfortable."

"What did I say about good behavior?"

I rolled my eyes then zipped my lips shut.

"Good boy."

We headed to the table near the back, and I spotted the woman who must be her friend. Her head was down as she looked at her phone. She had long, blonde hair set in open curls, and she wore a gray sweater with gold bracelets around her wrist.

As we edged closer, I noticed the purse on the chair beside her. It was deep purple and Coach, reminding me of a purse I'd seen before but couldn't remember where. There was a low burning candle on the table, and a full basket of bread—thankfully.

"Hey!" Taylor got to the table first and greeted her friend.

She looked up and set her eyes on Taylor. They were bright blue and icy—frozen just like her heart. Her hair was behind her shoulders, like it usually was. Her eye shadow was heavy, showing dark shades that made them appear smoky. Her voice was exactly the same as I remembered. "About time, girl."

"Sorry," Taylor said. "We're always late to everything."

I froze in place because my mind couldn't understand what I was looking at. I was two years in the past, looking at the woman I thought I would spend my life with. Not once had I run into her because this city was a big place. But now I was face-to-face with her, feeling the anger bubble and froth out of my ears. Even after all that time, I still hated her. I loathed everything about her, from her hair to the sound of her annoying voice. She still wore expensive things, from designer purses to exclusive jewelry.

I walked into that restaurant expecting a nice meal, but instead, I walked into my worst nightmare. When Taylor told me about her best friend, not once did I think this was a possibility. Sara was a common name. I'd already dated three of them.

I didn't know what to do. My first instinct told me to turn around and walk away before she looked at me. My life had been so much better since that night I walked away from her. I dumped her in the coldest way possible. I never told her the truth, that I caught her red-handed, sticking her tongue down some other guy's throat.

The anger came back, making my hands curl into fists.

Taylor didn't notice anything because her back was turned to me. "Sara, this is the man I've been telling you about for over a year now." She stepped away and turned to me, a smile on her face.

Sara laid her eyes on me, and she immediately went pale. All the blood drained from her face, and it was clear this was a nightmare for her just as it was for me. Her lips parted slightly like she wanted to gasp but didn't have the breath to achieve it. She didn't blink once as she stared at me, reliving the same relationship that I recalled.

I stared back, hating every expression on her face. I found her hideous now, absolutely appalling. What did I see in her all those years ago? What did I find so infatuating? She was a stupid girl who cared about stupid things. She was always looking for the next opportunity, side kicking anything that became obsolete—and that included me.

I hated her.

Hate was a strong word, but it was appropriate.

Taylor stared back and forth between us, expecting one of us to say hi or at least move. "Uh…do you two know each other?"

I refused to speak. My lips were tightly shut and my shoulders were tense. If I let my mouth open, I would say some horrifying things. It was better if I stayed quiet, not allowing my insults to escape.

"Muriel?" Sara whispered.

I hated it when she said my name. Not only did I hate her voice, but that name was just stupid. Why the fuck did my parents give it to me? My brother got a normal name, and I got my grandfather's name.

"What?" Taylor asked.

Sara examined my features, confirming who I was even when I didn't answer her question. It took a moment for the shock to dissipate, for her to understand this wasn't a sick dream. "He's Muriel...my ex."

Taylor still didn't get it. She stared at her friend as she processed what she said. "No...his name is Volt. Are you drunk?"

"Volt?" Sara asked. "That's not his name."

We continued to stand together in the restaurant, and we were drawing more attention to ourselves from the nearby tables. I wanted to walk out and never see this cunt again. But I didn't want to leave unless Taylor was with me.

Taylor turned to me, connecting the dots. "Volt isn't your real name...it's your middle name." She remembered what I told her so long ago. It seemed like a different lifetime.

I still hadn't said anything because I was too angry. I never wanted to see Sara again but now I was face-to-face with her. All the hatred and humiliation came back. Why did I love someone so unworthy of a single care?

"So..." Taylor didn't finish the sentence because she didn't know how.

"He was the one who broke up with me a few years ago." Sara dropped her gaze, clearly still hurting over the way I left her.

Now Taylor understood, understanding exactly what she was dealing with.

I didn't want to stand there a moment longer. I didn't want to look at that stupid whore as she played the victim. I was the one who got hurt. I was the one with a ring in my pocket while she fucked her ex.

I was done with this.

I turned around and walked out, unable to stare at her face a second longer than I had to. Why was Taylor friends with such a lying bitch? Why was this happening to me? Why was I about to marry a woman who was best friends with my ex?

I would never escape her.

Chapter Twelve

Taylor

Sara watched Volt leave the restaurant before she fell into the chair. A dazed look stretched across her face, unable to believe whom she just saw. Her eyes were still wide apart, trying to process endless information in nanoseconds.

I continued to stand near the table, just as confused. I walked in with Volt, expecting a fun dinner with my best friend, but instead, I walked into a soap opera. Sara told me about her ex and how much she loved him. He just walked out without an explanation.

And it was Volt.

There was a bottle of wine on the table so I sat across from her and immediately helped myself to a glass, knowing I would need it to get through this circus.

Sara didn't speak, her eyes trained on the door like Volt may return.

I downed one glass in a few seconds before I poured another.

Sara didn't reach for the bottle. She was stunned into silence.

"What are the odds?" This city was enormous, and we were best friends. How did we date the same guy but never figure it out? How did we both love the same guy but never realize it?

"I don't know." She finally spoke, her voice coming out weak. "He never liked his name. I'm not surprised he changed it."

Muriel didn't fit Volt at all. I couldn't even get myself to call him that. That was the name of someone I didn't know.

"This is insane." I didn't know what to say. I kept expecting myself to wake up. I wanted to pinch myself to speed up the process, but I knew it wouldn't work. This was real. And it was going to stay real.

"I know…" She finally moved and poured herself a glass of wine. She swirled it before she took a sip.

"I'm sorry," she whispered.

"Why are you sorry?" I asked. "You didn't do anything wrong?" No one did anything wrong. It was just a really strange coincidence.

"You were going to move in with him, and I know you love him…"

I *was* going to move in with him? Why was this past tense?

"And now everything is ruined."

"Why is everything ruined?" I admit it was weird, but we could get through it.

She sipped her wine before she gave me a cold look. "Because I was with him for over a year. Because I was in love with him. Because he broke my heart. Or do you not remember any of this?"

"No, I do. But that was two years ago, Sara."

"What does that matter?" she snapped. "You aren't supposed to date your friend's ex."

"I didn't know he was your ex."

"And I get that, but now you do know. And we're best friends. How is this supposed to work? He and I can never be in the same room together. We can never do stuff together. I can never come to your wedding. Don't you see how big of a problem this is?"

"Well...yeah." But I never expected it to come to this. "But don't you think the two of you could work this out? Volt and I have already been together for a year. We're moving in together. We want to get married someday. I can't just erase all these feelings we've developed for each other."

"Taylor, I had the exact same feelings." She poked herself hard in the chest, tears moving into her eyes. "I was devastated when he left. I thought he was going to propose and we were going to live happily ever after. How do you think it makes me feel to know he's moved on with someone else? Especially you."

My mouth fell slack because I was speechless. I didn't think about any of that.

She leaned back into the chair and crossed her arms over her chest, her eyes blinking quickly to dispel the moisture. "I know you're happy with him, and I don't want to ruin your happiness, but...this isn't something we can just ignore. This isn't going to work. We're best friends forever, so we always come first."

"So...you want me to break up with him?"

"It's not about want," she said. "There's no other option here."

"But I'm asking what you want me to do, Sara. Is that what you want?"

She looked away and avoided the question. After several breaths, she spoke. "If it were me, I'd break up with him."

"What?" I asked incredulously. "I'm sorry, but I can't picture that."

"I would," she argued. "I know I can be selfish sometimes, but we're best friends. This is forever. Guys will come and go, but we'll always be here. Muriel isn't some guy I just had a fling with. We had a relationship together. We loved each other. How could I possibly be okay with this? I'd be lying if I said I was."

I knew she was right. Deep in my heart, I knew.

"You of all people know how devastated I was. When you moved here, I was still getting over it."

I did know.

"Realistically, how is this going to work? Because I can't be around him. I can't handle seeing you two together. I can't handle the idea of the two of you being together... It's my worst nightmare."

I heard everything she said and it all made sense. "But...I love him." Our relationship was a slow burn. It took us a long time to figure out exactly how we felt. We started off as best friends and slowly fell in love, not even realizing it. And when we did finally come together, it was the most beautiful thing. When we broke up, I was absolutely devastated. I couldn't live without him, not after he made me so happy. "Sara, I love you. But...I can't imagine my life without him. I want to marry him. He's my best friend."

"I know. I know that better than anyone." She gave me a sympathetic look. "But...tell me how else it could work."

I didn't have a single answer.

"The only way it will work is if we stop being friends. Is that what you want?"

"Why do we have to stop being friends?" Why was she making me choose?

"Because we can't be ourselves. I could never ask you about him. If you had kids, I could never look at them. There would be a huge hole in our relationship and it would be awkward and strange. You really don't see where I'm coming from?"

"No, I do. I just...you're asking me to give up the love of my life."

"He was the love of my life too, Taylor." She gave me a cold look. "Believe me, I understand everything you're feeling. I felt all of that before he walked out on me. Even now, I'm still not over it. Knowing he asked you to move in when he never asked me that...is excruciating."

I looked out the window just to avoid eye contact. This evening was supposed to be different. It was supposed to be fun. My best friend and my boyfriend were supposed to get along. We weren't supposed to talk about me leaving him. "I can't see myself with anyone else, Sara."

"And neither can I. I haven't been in a relationship since."

"Are you telling me you're still in love with him?" It'd been two years. She couldn't be.

She shrugged. "When you love someone once, you never stop loving them. If I feel this way for him, he must feel this way for me. Don't you think that will be a problem, having the two of us together? I'm not saying I would ever betray you like that, but he and I could develop feelings for each other again and something might happen. So many things could go wrong in this scenario. The three of us are never going to be able to make this work."

That evidence was even more painful.

"I'm sorry, Taylor," she whispered. "But I don't see how this works...unless we stop being friends. You don't want that, right? Our parents are friends, and we've known each other since we were in diapers. Isn't our relationship more important than what you have with him? With any guy?"

"Yes...but he's my best friend too. We've loved each other for a long time. It's not like it's easy for me to just cut him out. You guys are both equally important to me."

Her eyes fell. "I'm sorry. But that's the way it is."

I crossed my arms over my chest, feeling the depression creep in.

"You know I'm right."

I didn't want to listen to it—not right now. "Just give me some time, okay? This is a lot of information to get in thirty minutes. I woke up this morning thinking my life was a certain way, and now it's been turned on its head."

"I get it," she whispered.

How could I ever let Volt go? He was such an important person in my life now. Arguably, I was closer to him than I was to her. When she settled down and got married, she would understand. But I couldn't lose her either. We'd known each other forever. She was family.

What was I supposed to do?

***

When I came home, all the lights were off in the apartment. I knew Volt was home, drinking whiskey in a dark corner somewhere. His wallet and keys were on the table in the entryway.

I didn't call out for him because he wouldn't respond.

I walked into this office because I knew that's where he would be. Floor-to-ceiling windows took up the back wall, and he sat in the office chair as he faced the city lights. A bottle of whiskey sat on the counter along with a bowl of fresh ice cubes.

He didn't want to talk. He made that clear.

But I didn't want to be alone.

I walked inside and came around the desk, waiting for him to react to me.

He took a drink.

I stood beside him and turned my gaze to the burning lights of the city. You could see everything from up there. Central Park was lit up with street lamps but it was dark in comparison to the rest of the city.

He took another drink, silently dismissing me.

Whenever I had a problem, I ran to Volt. I told him everything, and he gave me advice. That was our relationship. But now I couldn't run to him. And I couldn't run to Sara either.

I moved onto his lap and straddled his hips, wanting to be close to him. My arms moved around his neck, and I pulled up my dress so it wouldn't stretch over my ass.

He held the drink in one hand but the other rested on my ass. He didn't make eye contact with me but he didn't ask me to get off either.

I wanted to talk and have him make me feel better. But I didn't know what to say and neither did he. The entire situation was terrible. The only thing we could do together was move.

I undid his jeans then pulled down his boxers underneath. His cock popped out but it was soft. I ran my hand up and down his length, and within seconds, it came to life.

He set his glass down, his breathing increasing.

I pulled my thong over and inserted him inside me. I should be repulsed that he slept with my best friend. I should be disgusted that he'd been inside her and now he was inside me. But I didn't feel that way. I still loved him—madly.

This was the only comfort I could find. This was the only form of communication I knew how to use. I returned my arms around his neck and bounced up and down, taking his cock over and over.

His hands went to my ass and he breathed with me as we moved together. Quiet moans escaped our lips and our breathing grew heavier, full of lust and undeniable love.

It made me feel better, made me feel close to him again. We fell into our usual groove, moving together in just the right way. He made me moan more times than I could count. The chair rocked back and forth from our shifting weight, and my pussy soaked his shaft from tip to base.

We didn't say a word to each other, expressing our love for one another as we moved. His lips brushed past mine before he gave me a soft kiss that defied how aggressively we took each other. I kissed him back, needing his mouth on mine to wash away the pain.

He gripped my ass and moved me down his length harder, stretching me farther apart as his dick became swollen with desperation. He lost himself in me, taking everything and giving it back for my own pleasure.

It went on forever, neither one of us coming because we didn't want it to end. We just kept moving, not thinking about anything else but each other. We fell deeper into each other, our hearts beating in sync. I didn't want this moment to end and neither did he.

So we kept going.

***

We didn't speak to each other.

In fact, we didn't say a single word.

Neither one of us were ready to talk about what happened that night. The conversation wouldn't go anywhere we wanted. It was simply too painful, too heartbreaking.

He gave me a kiss before he went to work, and I kissed him back.

But we never said goodbye.

At work, I didn't concentrate. My thoughts were constantly all over the place, replaying everything Sara said to me. How would this ever work between us? The three of us could never be friends. Not when they had such a deep history together. Eventually, I would have to choose. But whom would I pick?

When I came home, he was already there. He sat on the couch and watched TV but made no move to speak to me. He didn't even look at me. The apartment was unnaturally quiet when we had nothing to say. It was like no one lived there at all.

I headed into the bedroom and removed my heels. They were killing my feet, and I longed for the isolation. It was hard to think when other people were constantly in your presence.

Volt walked through the door and came behind me. When he placed his hand on my hip, I knew why he was there. He wanted to be with me, but he didn't want to talk. His mouth never opened as he lifted my dress over my head and snapped my bra off. He dragged my panties down then directed me onto the bed, my ass in the air.

Our sex life changed after that dinner. We were never so aggressive and physical when we made love. But now, we fucked like animals, taking all our feelings out on each other. He didn't want me to go so he possessed me harder, ramming his dick inside me so he would never forget I was his.

That I was always his.

***

After we showered, we went out to dinner. There were no groceries in the house, and we needed something otherwise we would starve. But we didn't talk about having dinner. We just assumed the same thought at the same time.

We sat across from each other at the table and waited for our food to arrive. We still hadn't spoken to one another. We entertained ourselves by looking at each other. He looked into my eyes like I wasn't there. He stared all he wanted, enjoying the comfort he found.

I did the same thing, cherishing the strength of his shoulders and the way his powerful chest bulged against his t-shirt. His hair was a little messy since he didn't bother styling it after showering. But his laziness was somehow sexy.

He sipped his wine before he stirred it, his eyes never leaving mine. He'd been drinking a lot more since that terrible night. In fact, it was rare to see him without a drink in his hand—unless he was fucking me.

Dinner finally arrived and we ate quietly together. To an outsider, we probably looked deaf, unable to hear each other so we just ate in silence. Or maybe we just looked pissed at each other.

After dinner, we went to the grocery store and picked out the things we needed so we wouldn't starve in the apartment. He threw in a lot of whiskey and gin, along with a few beers.

I didn't say anything.

We went home and put everything away. Once that was done, there was nothing else for us to do. Unless we sat together and had a conversation, the night would be over.

But when I looked at him, I knew he wasn't ready to talk.

Neither was I.

Volt scooped me up and laid me across the kitchen table. He quickly pulled down his jeans and boxers and lifted up my dress. My panties were gone in an instant, and he was inside me a second later.

I didn't want it easy. I wanted it rough. I wanted him to fuck all my problems away. Instead of fighting, we chose to do this. It was just as aggressive and harsh, but it felt a lot better than screaming at one another.

He leaned over the table and gave me a slow kiss.

I wrapped my arms tightly around him and dug my fingers into his hair. What we had was so incredible, and I never wanted to lose it. I loved the way he looked at me. I loved the way he made love to me.

I loved everything.

A week went by and we still didn't talk about the dark clouds looming over our heads. We spent our time together in comfortable silence or engaging in our preferred activity of fucking.

But it went on long enough, and we'd come to a fork in the road neither one of us could ignore. We had to talk about it, to discuss what happened that night and what we were going to do about it—if we were going to do anything.

I came home and spotted him on the couch.

When he heard me come inside, he set his whiskey down and stood up, undoing his tie and his shirt so he could get right down to the good stuff.

I almost let it go on. "Volt, we need to talk."

He froze on the spot, letting his tie dangle around his neck.

"I don't want to talk about it either, but we can't do this forever."

"I can do it forever."

I set my things down then joined him on the couch. I wasn't even sure what to say because I hadn't rehearsed it. I'd never been in a situation where I couldn't work out the solution. But this problem simply wasn't solvable.

He sighed and sat beside me, his body tensing in irritation. He darkened into a man I didn't recognize. "What's there to say?"

"Sara and I talked after you left."

"Your point?" he said harshly. "We broke up two years ago. She's practically a stranger to me now. What does it matter?"

"It matters because she and I are best friends."

He rubbed his knuckles.

"This is a problem for us. And you know it is."

"It'll go away," he said. "Just give it some time, and it will pass."

"What will pass?"

"I don't know...the tension?" He rubbed his chin, fidgeting in place because he couldn't sit still.

"Volt, Sara has been my best friend since I can remember. The fact the two of you used to love each other presents a problem for us."

"Not really," he said. "It was a long time ago."

"But not for her. How can we keep our friendship if you've been with both of us?"

He shrugged. "Just tell her to get over it."

"Volt." I warned him with my tone. "I don't want to have this conversation any more than you do, but knock off the attitude."

He ran his fingers through his hair, releasing an irritated sigh.

"I don't know what to do."

"I don't know what that means," he said quietly. "There's nothing you can do. It's in the past. It's been done."

"I mean what I should do now. Sara is my best friend."

"Again, I don't know what that means. It's going to take some time to get used to, but if we're all mature about it, we'll be fine."

Now I understood why he didn't get what I was saying. "Volt, that's not how it's going to work. Only one of you can stay."

"What's that supposed to mean?"

How could I put it into terms he would understand? "If you started seeing a girl that Derek had already been in a relationship with, would you keep seeing her?"

"No."

"Now do you understand?"

"But if I just started seeing her, I wouldn't have a problem dumping her. But if I'd been with her for a year and I was in love with her, it would be different. I would tell Derek to get over it."

"But isn't that breaking the friend code? Dating your friend's ex?"

"Yeah. But you didn't know I was her ex. It's not the same thing at all."

"She doesn't see it that way."

He froze on the spot, his hands flinching. The weight of the situation dawned on him. "Wait. She told you to stop seeing me?" He turned to me, the anger deep in his eyes.

"In so many words..."

He shook his head, clenching his jaw. "That fucking cunt."

"Whoa." I held up my hand. "That's my friend you're badmouthing."

"She is a cunt, and I don't feel bad for saying it. I can't believe she said that to you."

"She made valid points. How will the three of us ever hang out?"

"Why do we have to hang out at all?" he snapped. "Why can't you two go spend time together, and I'll just stay out of it? Don't bring me up at all. We've been together for a year, and she didn't even know."

"What about when we get married someday?" I asked. "She's not going to come to the wedding?"

"It's one day. She'll live."

"And when we have kids?"

"She can spend time with them when it's just you and her."

He had an excuse for everything. "She can't handle the idea of us being together. She can't stand the thought of us moving in together and having a serious relationship. It hurts. I have to say, if the situation were reversed, I would feel the same way."

"Well, that's ludicrous. She really expects you to leave me for her?"

"It's not like that," I explained. "It's just...how will this ever work? Our relationship will never be the same."

"It'll never be the same anyway," he argued. "You've already slept with the same guy. You've already loved the same guy. The damage is done, Taylor. Breaking us up isn't going to change anything."

I dropped my hands in my lap and eyed my blue fingernail polish. This conversation was more difficult than

I imagined. There was no way to fix it, no way to make it right. Even if I found a solution, it wasn't ideal. "That's why I have to end it with one of you."

He turned to me, a crazed look in his eye. "I think Sara is a stupid bitch, alright? But I wouldn't want you to stop being friends with her because of what happened between us. And she better not want to ruin your happiness with me just because of her problems with our old relationship. What kind of friend would she be to ask that of you?"

"It's not about her asking me," I explained. "It's about knowing our friendship will never be the same. It'll be strained and awkward, and we'll eventually drift apart and stop talking altogether. I don't want that."

"And you can break up with me?" he asked incredulously.

"No." I grabbed his thigh. "I don't want that either."

"Then back to my original point. The three of us can make this work. I'm not saying it'll be easy or something I even want to do, but I'll do it for you."

I knew that wasn't going to work. Sara made her feelings about the situation very clear. She wouldn't be able to handle Volt and I being together, moving in together or getting married one day. "That's not going to work...I told you that."

"Then what?" he demanded.

"She's my best friend. No one knows me better than she does. I can't just cut her out of my life. I don't want to be that person who chooses a boyfriend over a best friend. I don't want to hurt her."

"What are you saying?" he whispered.

"I don't know..." I didn't want to say it out loud. It was too painful.

He left the couch and rose to his full height, looking down at me in anger. "You're actually thinking about ending this?" The hurt in his voice was mixed with the ferocity.

"Volt—"

"No. That's not an option. You aren't going to break up with me just because she has a problem with us. Tell her to go to hell."

I came to my feet. "What if this was Derek? Would you be able to cut him out of your life?"

"No. But he wouldn't force me to make a choice."

"But if he did," I pressed. "What would you do? Would you turn away from your friend that has been there for you through everything? Could you really do that to someone you love?"

"Could you end a relationship with the love of your life?" He threw his fist into his chest, making a loud thud. "Could you really end this when we both know it's going to last forever? Can you really walk away from me?"

My eyes watered in frustration. I didn't know what to do. Either way, I lost. "I'm just explaining that it's a really difficult decision. I don't know what to do."

"Breaking up with me isn't the solution, Taylor."

"I know...but neither is ending my relationship with her."

He put his hands on his hips and slowly started to pace. "I'm not letting you end this. That's not an option. She goes, I don't."

I couldn't do that. I couldn't do that to my best friend. "She's family, Volt."

"What the fuck am I?" he hissed. "I'm living with you. I sleep with you every night. I'm going have children with you. I'm your damn family." Spit flew out of his mouth he was so angry. His face tinted red and the vein in his forehead throbbed. "How could possibly pick her over me?"

"Would you pick me over Derek?"

"Don't flip the conversation."

"I'm not flipping it." I stomped my foot, unable to do anything else to express my anger. "I'm just making a point. I know how much Derek means to you. What if you had to choose him over me?"

"Would never happen."

"But if it did. Who would you choose?"

He looked away, his eyes still angry.

"Exactly. It's not an easy decision. It's damn hard."

"I would choose you, Taylor. If the situations were exactly the same, I would choose you."

"Whatever," I snapped. "It's easy to say when you aren't in the situation."

"All I know is, I can't live without you." He dropped his hands to his sides. "Plain and simple."

My eyes watered further, hating those sweet words at a time like this.

"I understand she's your friend—"

"Best friend. Nat is just a friend. Sara is a lot more."

"Whatever," he said. "But friends come and go—"

"Boyfriends come and go."

Threat entered his eyes. "I'm not a boyfriend, and we both know it. I wouldn't have asked you to move in with me if I were just your boyfriend. I don't have a name for it, but I'm a lot more important than that. So, don't downplay this."

"I'm not."

"Don't pick her." He came closer to me, his body vibrating with rage. "I'm not going to let you pick her."

"You have no idea how difficult this is…"

"I'm not letting you walk away from this. I'm not letting you turn your back on us. If you think I'm going to let you leave and marry some other guy, you're sadly mistaken." He turned around and threw the coffee table, making the glass top shatter. He grabbed his jacket on the way to the door then stormed out. When he slammed the door, the sound reverberated through the apartment.

I'm pretty sure his neighbors heard it.

Chapter Thirteen

Volt

"We're closing, man." He swiped my card for the drinks I bought and tossed it back to me.

"Isn't it a little early to close?" I'd been sitting at the counter for a few hours. It wasn't even midnight.

"It's five."

"PM?" I asked incredulously.

"It's five in the morning, idiot," the bartender snapped. "How drunk are you?"

I shrugged and downed the rest of my glass so he wouldn't take it away from me.

"You need me to call you a cab?"

"I'll walk." I snatched my debit card and stumbled out, feeling dizzy. I fumbled for the door and made it to the sidewalk. They locked the doors behind me, and I saw people heading to work as they marched past. A lot of joggers were out, exercising before starting the day.

I was so drunk, I slid to the ground and leaned against the wall. I looked like a bum with an expensive jacket. People didn't pay any attention to me as they passed, writing me off as a nobody.

My phone started to ring, so I pulled it out and looked at the screen. My vision was blurry, and I couldn't make anything out. It might have said Taylor's name but I wasn't totally sure. I answered it anyway. "Wad up, dog?"

Taylor's concerned voice came over the line. "Volt?"

"Bark bark."

"Are you okay?"

"Moo…" I laughed for some strange reason.

"You're wasted, aren't you?"

"What's it to you, chicka?"

She sighed into the phone. "Where are you?"

"I don't know," I said with a shrug.

"Get home now. I'm worried."

"But not too worried, right?" I snapped. "Since you're willing to pick that stupid bitch over me."

"Volt, stop calling her that."

"I'll call her whatever the hell I want." Click. I hung up on her. I was playing with fire and I knew it, but I was too drunk to care.

My phone rang a few moments later, and I knew it was Taylor. She wanted to give me an earful about my poor behavior. "Look, you have your opinion, and I have mine. She's a bitch. I have every right to say it."

"Dude, it's Derek." His voice was raspy like he just rolled out of bed.

"Oh, hi." He was the last person I expected. "Why are you calling me?"

"Taylor told me you're being a little bitch."

"What?" I shrieked. "I'm the one being a bitch?" She really had some nerve. That dumb ho Sara was the real culprit.

"Where are you?" he said. "I'm going to swing by and pick you up."

"I'm good. Go back to sleep."

"I'm coming for you whether you like it or not. Now tell me where you are."

"I don't even know…"

"Look around, idiot."

I turned back to the bar I was just in. "Tito's…I think it says Tito's."

"Did you go there because that's where you caught Sara cheating on you?"

How did he remember that? "I don't know. I honestly don't remember how I got here."

"I'll come get you. Hang tight."

"I'm the bum sleeping against the wall."

"Yeah, I'll figure it out. You'll be the only asshole drunk at five am."

***

Derek walked me inside the apartment, my arm around his shoulder. He supported my weight with his since my legs were Jell-O. I drank more last night than I had in my entire life.

I was going to hurl.

"Thank god." Taylor helped him get me to the couch. "Thank you so much, Derek."

"No problem." He dropped me on the couch then stretched his back. "That fucker weighs a lot."

I meant to flip him off but extended my forefinger instead.

"Idiot," Derek whispered under his breath.

"Thanks for bringing him home," Taylor said. "He wouldn't tell me where he was."

"Bad fight, huh?" he asked.

"She's dumping me," I blurted. "Fucking dumping me." I lay on my back and stared at the ceiling, feeling my eyes close.

"Uh…" Derek looked at her, assuming it couldn't possibly be true.

"We'll talk about it later," she whispered to him. "It's complicated."

"Not really," I said. "Her best friend is Sara. The same Sara I used to date. There. Pretty simple."

Derek's eyes widened. "Wow…that's a coincidence."

"Now she wants to pick her over me." I crossed my arms over my chest. "She'd rather keep her best friend and kiss me goodbye. That's some fucked up shit, huh?"

Derek stared at her again.

"That's not correct," Taylor explained. "It's just messy."

"Tell yourself whatever you want to hear." I was being a huge ass but whatever. I could blame it on the alcohol.

"I'm gonna go…" Derek headed to the door. "Let me know if he needs anything else."

"I'll take it from here," Taylor said. "Thanks for getting up."

"No problem. I'm going back to bed now." He walked out. "Bye, Volt." He shut the door without waiting for me to respond.

I closed my eyes because I couldn't stay awake anymore. My mind was in a cloud of confusion.

Taylor removed my shoes and socks then pulled my jacket off. She removed my pants next, unzipping them and dragging them down my hips.

"You aren't getting any from me tonight."

"Shut up, Volt." She got my pants off then removed my shirt. When I was just in boxers, she covered me with a blanket and placed a pillow under my head. Like old times, she grabbed two painkillers and set them on the table next to a glass of water. "I have to get ready for work."

"Good. Don't come back." Hatred flew out of my mouth, but I couldn't stop it. I was so angry. I finally had what I wanted, and it was being taken away from me. "Take your shirt and leave. I don't want you anymore." I couldn't stop myself. I just kept going.

Taylor hid the hurt look on her face and walked down the hallway. The shower started to run as she got ready for work.

Instead of falling asleep, I just laid there. I hated myself for everything I just said. I hated myself for leaving last night. My sorrow took charge and put all my reasoning aside.

She walked to the entryway thirty minutes later, ready to head off to work. She had her big bag full of her books and notepads. She didn't bother saying goodbye to me. She didn't even look at me.

If I didn't say something now, I would regret it forever. "Baby?"

Her feet flinched by the entryway. I couldn't see her, but I could hear her.

"I'm sorry. I didn't mean any of that. I love you, and I don't want you to leave. Not now. Not ever."

She didn't move. Her feet remained glued to the ground. Maybe she would just walk out because she was sick of my shit. Maybe there was no going back. Maybe it was too late to apologize.

Then her heels headed my way, tapping against the hardwood floor. She came to my side and sat at the edge of the cushion, her hair done in nice curls and her makeup looking natural.

I looked up at her, hoping she still loved me.

She placed her hand on my chest and rubbed me gently. Then she leaned in and kissed me.

In that moment, it seemed like everything would be okay. She still loved me. She still wanted me. At the end of the day, she would still come home to me. We could get through this.

"Get some sleep."

"Okay. Love you."

"Love you too."

***

I just got out of the shower when she came home. My clothes smelled like booze and dirt, and even a session at the dry cleaner wouldn't save my sport coat. That thing was ruined.

I'd have to buy another one.

"Hey." I greeted her at the entryway, grateful she still came home to me after my breakdown last night. When I was able to think again, I realized I acted out because I was scared.

Scared of losing her.

"Hey." She set her things down and gave me a soft kiss.

"Sorry about last night...and this morning."

"It's okay, Volt. I know you didn't mean the things you said."

Well, I meant the part about Sara being a bitch. "I got carried away with everything. I've lost you once, and I can't do it again. I was just afraid, not that it's an excuse."

"It's a really stressful time for both of us. I know what you're feeling."

Now we were back to where we started. The problem still loomed over our heads like a raincloud. It would hover there until it finally poured down on us. All the anxiety crept back into my veins, making me sick. "Just tell me we'll work through this. Tell me it's you and me. I can't deal with this anymore unless I have that reassurance."

Instead of giving it to me, she just stared.

"Baby..."

"Honestly, I don't know what's going to happen. I can't ignore this and hope it'll go away. I can't just pretend this isn't a serious problem. Because it is. I don't have an answer for you."

She was breaking my heart. "You're actually considering ending this relationship?" It hurt just to say it out loud. In fact, it killed me.

"I'm considering everything."

I wanted to break the already broken coffee table. I wanted to demolish everything in the apartment. I wanted to scream until every window shattered. "How can you possibly even think that?"

"Just listen to me."

I didn't think I could listen to her insanity.

"Sara has been my best friend my whole life—"

"You've already told me that."

"Listen to me," she snapped. "I can't picture my life without her. We've gone through so much together. When I'm old and gray, she'll still be my friend. She'll still be there for me. She'll be the godmother to my children. I know you don't like her and can't understand how much she means to me, but she means the world to me."

I had a mouthful of hateful things to say but I kept them back.

"And then there's you..."

"What about me?"

"You're my best friend. You're everything to me. You're the love of my life. When I think about my future, you're always the man I see. Even before we were anything serious, I saw you at the end of my road. You're the father of my kids. You're the man I grow old with." Her eyes tore up in sadness. "Don't you see it?"

"See what?" I whispered.

"How important both of you are to me? The two of you are equals. How am I supposed to choose when I love you both so much?" She sniffed and quickly wiped her tears away, trying to mask her overwhelming sadness. "What am I supposed to do, Volt? If you have any objective advice, I'd love to hear it."

"I don't. I just want you to choose me." She was essential to my happiness. Without her, I was nothing. I thought I reached the end of the road with her. I thought I said goodbye to a life of bitterness and loneliness.

"I know."

"I need to think about it. I need some time."

"Okay." I couldn't sway her in either direction. I already tried but failed.

"I'm going to go back to my place."

What? "Why?"

"I need to be alone for a while. I can't think clearly when I'm with you all the time."

I hated this. Loathed it. I didn't give her my blessing because she didn't have it. I remained silent.

"I just need a few days."

Even a single night was too long.

"I'm going to gather my things..." She walked around me, being careful not to brush against my arm.

I listened to her go, resisting the urge to grab her and force her to stay. It took all my strength not to fight her. It took all my strength to stand by and do nothing.

It took everything I had.

Chapter Fourteen

Taylor

Being in my apartment felt oddly lonely.

It used to be my home, my shelter. But now, when I thought of home, I thought of Volt's place. I missed his king size bed and the king who slept in it every night. I missed the smell of his aftershave in the bathroom. I missed the sound of whiskey filling a glass.

My apartment was just quiet.

Now, it was too small even though it was just for me. My boxes were scattered around everywhere, and I spent most of my time drinking wine on the couch. I stared at the window at my crappy view of the adjacent building and tried to find the answer to my problem.

Every time I picked someone, I couldn't stick with the decision. I flipped back to the other person, making my justifications for that choice. But it kept shifting back and forth, never remaining permanent.

I thought I could live without Sara. When I was happy with Volt, the person I spent most of my time with anyway, did I really need her in my life anymore? Would I be able to go on without having a best girlfriend to talk to? But then I pictured my wedding and how strange it would feel without her standing beside me. I pictured giving birth to my kids and how strange it would be not having her in the room with me. Could I really live that kind of future?

But then I pictured my life without Volt. Sara would be there for me through anything, and she would be my maid of honor at my wedding. But whom would I be marrying? Would I be in love with him? Or would I just settle because I could never get over Volt? When I pictured my kids, they had his eyes and his good heart. How would that ever happen if I didn't end up with him?

There was no right answer.

No matter what I picked, I lost.

I would regret either decision I made.

Sara texted me just as I finished my bottle of wine. *Haven't heard from you in a while. Are you okay?*

I didn't text her back. I just stared at the message.

I know you're reading this. I'm going to call you in five minutes so be prepared.

How did she know stuff like that?

Right on cue, she called. "Hey."

"Hi." I didn't know what to say to her. I hadn't made a decision yet so there was nothing to talk about.

"You sound down."

"Well, I'm pretty depressed. Makes sense." I shoved the glass into my face and took a long drink.

"Did you break up with Volt?"

I wanted to lie just to make her happy but I couldn't. "No..."

"When are you going to break up with him?"

"I never said I was."

"It didn't seem like it at the restaurant. We both agreed there was no other way."

I didn't want to lose him. He was the perfect guy. "Sara, can you please just make an effort to make this work? If we just started dating, I would stop seeing him. But I'm already in love with him. Not boring love. Like, I want him to give me a big fat ring kind of love."

"Don't make me the bad guy, Tay. I was in love with him too. I wanted to marry him too. You know how bummed I was when he left me. There's no way you forgot about it that quickly."

"I haven't..."

"I didn't just have a meaningless fling with this guy. I loved him. He loved me. You expect me to just get over that? To give you my blessing? No woman would be able to do that."

"And no woman came make a decision like this."

"Look, if you want to be with him, I can understand. He's pretty great. I wouldn't hold it against you. But I'd definitely have to bow out."

My heart sagged in sadness.

"I can't see you together. I can't stand beside you on your big day and pretend to be happy for you. I just can't." Her sadness seeped over the phone. "I really wish I could, but I can't. I'm sorry."

"It's okay. I understand."

"But I don't think you'd be truly happy with him without me. Every girl needs her best friend. Who would you go shopping with? Who would you do stuff with? When he's not around, who will you hang out with? Our parents won't be able to spend time together anymore either. And frankly, I'd be hurt if you picked a guy over me. We've been friends forever, and you've known him for, like, a year."

"It may be a short amount of time, but what we have is real."

"I know," she whispered. "But...I always thought I was on a different level. You're willing to throw away our friendship for him?"

"I just... I don't know." This was so fucking hard.

"You know what decision you should make. It's just hard to do it. I get it."

"And what decision is that?"

She sighed into the phone. "You need to break up with him."

***

After a week had come and gone, I finally went to his apartment. I was surprised he didn't call me in that amount of time. Maybe he was dreading our forthcoming conversation.

Maybe he knew what decision I'd made.

I didn't use my key to get inside. Instead, I knocked. I didn't want to frighten him by barging inside. As far as I knew, I wouldn't be living there anymore. The weight of reality fell on my shoulders, and I wasn't sure if I could go through with this.

I should just leave.

Volt opened the door and allowed me inside. He didn't greet me with a kiss or an affectionate embrace. He hardly looked at me.

The apartment was dark like it usually was. We rarely turned on the lights, and the only glow came from the TV in the background. It was on mute, but the pictures danced on the wall.

A bottle of whiskey sat on the new coffee table, along with a bowl of ice. He'd been drinking himself into silence, doing what he did best when he was depressed. He wore jeans and a t-shirt, his hard body looking nice in the clothing.

I didn't speak a word because I wasn't ready to.

Volt didn't look at me. He crossed his arms over his chest and stared into his kitchen. "This isn't happening."

I stared at his face and waited for an explanation.

"I'm not stupid. You wouldn't have knocked on the door like that unless you decided not to live here. And if you don't live here, that means you live somewhere else."

He took the words right out of my mouth, but that didn't make it less painful. He stripped the truth from me in silence without asking a single question. I wanted to say something to make this easier, but there wasn't a single thing I could say.

"You chose her." His voice turned cold, maniacal.

"Volt...I don't have any other choice."

"But you do have a choice," he snapped. "You're really going to throw us away because I dated your friend?

How is that right? She's not a real friend to make you choose."

"But she's right. This will never work."

"So, you're just going to move on with some other guy?" he hissed. "You're going to spend forever with someone else? How does that make sense?"

"It doesn't make sense." Tears sprang from my eyes immediately, pouring out and trailing down my cheeks. I couldn't keep them back because I was in too much pain. When I knew this conversation was coming, I prepared myself. I numbed myself. But now that it was happening, I couldn't hold my feelings in check. They spilled out and cascaded down my body.

"Taylor, this is wrong. It's a betrayal to everything we have."

"I know…but I don't know what else to do."

"Forget about her."

"I can't, Volt. She's my best friend. I can't walk away from someone I've known my entire life."

He stepped back, running his hand through his hair so he wouldn't punch something. "This is unbelievable."

"If it makes any difference, this is so hard for me. I hate this."

"No, it doesn't make a fucking difference," he snapped. "How can you choose her over me when she cheated on me? How is that fair? She betrayed me. She walked away from me. She tossed me aside like garbage. No, she doesn't get to treat me like shit and take away the woman I love. It's not gonna work like that."

I stared at him through my tears, listening to his rampage. "Sara is the one who cheated on you?"

"Yes," he snapped. "I told you that."

I guess I didn't put the pieces together.

"So how is that fair?" He threw his arms down. "She killed me once and now she's doing it again. That woman is a fucking terror."

The fact she cheated on him did make a difference. Volt left for a reason. If she didn't screw things up, they may have ended up together. But she threw him away, and that was her fault. "I'll talk to her."

"No."

"No, what?"

"Don't tell her why I really left. I never want her to get closure. I want her to always wonder what happened between us. If you tell her, then my revenge is ruined."

"But what's more important?" I asked. "Revenge or making us work?"

He stared at me in silence before he released a deep sigh.

"Volt?"

"Fine." He gave in. "Confront her."

"I will." I stared at him and felt the distance between us. We weren't officially over, but it felt that way. Even if she owned up to what she did, what difference would it make? But I had to try anyway. "I'll go talk to her now."

"Okay." He crossed his arms over his chest and leaned against the table. He turned his head away from me, not wanting to look at me as I left.

Maybe this would just make things harder in the end, but I walked up to him and planted a kiss on his lips. I felt his soft mouth move against mine slightly. He didn't want to kiss me back out of stubbornness, but he couldn't stop himself. He breathed into me, all his longing and desperation evident.

I pulled away before it turned into something more. I stopped it before he threw me on the table and took me right then and there. If that happened, I would be lost all over again.

***

"What did you want to talk about?" Sara opened the door for me then fell onto the couch. She had a glass of wine with a half empty bottle on the coffee table.

I sat on the other couch, unsure how to bring up this awkward subject.

"Did you break up with him yet?"

It was the second time she asked me, eager for me to get it done. Clearly, she didn't understand just how difficult it was. "There's something I want to talk about. It's about Volt."

She grabbed her glass of wine and rolled her eyes. "Girl, I know this is hard for you. But he and I are never going to make this work. It's that simple."

"I get that, Sara. But Volt told me something that changes the situation."

"What?" She set her glass down, intrigued.

"He said you cheated on him." I watched her expression, waiting to see her embarrassment and shame.

"What?" she shrieked. "I did no such thing."

"But he said—"

"Taylor, he's just saying what he needs to say to get you to stick around. I never, ever cheated on him. Why would I when I was in love with him? I swear to everything that's good on this earth that I never betrayed him. I even swear on our friendship."

Her words echoed around in my mind, and she said it with such emotion I believed her. She even swore on our friendship. Maybe what Volt saw was a mistake. Maybe it was just a misunderstanding.

"Why would I cheat on a great guy? You saw how miserable I was when he left me? A year later, I was still miserable."

"Yeah...you're right."

"I know you're trying to find a loophole in this, but there isn't one. I'm sorry."

I'm sorry too.

Chapter Fifteen

Volt

When Taylor came back to my apartment, I hoped she carried good news. The fact Sara cheated on me made all the difference in the world. She couldn't have it both ways. She couldn't treat me like shit then stop me from being happy two years later. "What happened?"

Instead of being happy, she seemed just as depressed. "She denied it."

"What?" My temples immediately pulsed in ferocity. My muscles contracted like I was about to enter a cage match. My refrigerator was about to be pushed to the ground and smashed into pieces.

"She swore on our friendship she never did. And I believe her. I mean, she wouldn't lie to me about that."

"But she did lie," I snapped. "I saw her."

"Maybe what you thought you saw wasn't what happened."

I clenched my hands into fists so I wouldn't snap. I didn't want to start a rampage when Taylor was so close to me. She was bound to get in the way and get hurt. I tried to control my body from striking, but it took all my strength not to. "I know what the fuck I saw."

"Volt—"

"No, you listen to me. I'm not an idiot. I know what a cheating slut looks like. How dare you take her side over mine."

"I'm not taking her side. I just think you should have confronted her all those years ago. Maybe there was a simple explanation. But since you never said anything, you'll never know."

"Well, I'll just go back in time and do that then."

She didn't have the patience for my sarcasm right now. "I don't know what happened two years ago, but Sara wouldn't lie to me."

"Why are you so sure about that?"

"Because she wouldn't. We never lie to each other."

"Did you ever think that maybe she's lying just to get you to break up with me?"

"What does she get out of that?"

"Payback."

"What?" She wasn't following.

"She's probably pissed that I left her and now I'm rich, even more sexy, and I treat you like a queen. She's jealous, Taylor. Plain and simple." It made perfect sense.

She never understood why I left, and now that I'm giving someone else everything she ever wanted, she pissed.

"But...she's not vindictive like that."

"Snap out of it." I snapped my fingers in front of her face. "I know you see the good in people, but pay attention to the bad too. This woman cheated on me so she has no problem lying to you. Why won't you believe me?"

"I never said I don't believe you. It's just hard for me to have an opinion about this when I wasn't there. She looked me in the eye and said she didn't cheat on you. What am I supposed to do? Call her a liar."

"Yes," he snapped. "That's exactly what you should do."

She took a step back, needing a break from this fight. "Volt, nothing has changed. It's still so messed up."

My anger died immediately, but disgust replaced it. "You can't be serious."

"It'll still never work."

"You're telling me that you're choosing someone who lies to you over me?" This couldn't be happening. This couldn't be real. Sara broke my heart two years ago. I spent my life sleeping with anything that moved just to get over what happened. Then Taylor walked into my life and fixed me. Now Sara is taking that away too? This woman was the fucking plague. She killed everything good in this world and turned it to ash.

I fucking hate her.

"She didn't lie to me, Volt."

"Well, I didn't lie either."

"I'm not saying you did," she whispered. "But maybe you didn't see what you thought you saw."

"It's pretty hard to see your girlfriend making out with some guy and then realize you were wrong—she was just giving him a high-five." How stupid did she think I was?

"I'm sorry." She headed to the door, walking away from me.

"This is it? This is how this ends?" I couldn't believe it. We were perfect just a few weeks ago. She was moving in with me. I was going to fucking marry her. And now she was walking out.

"Please don't make this harder..."

It was impossible to make this harder. It was already deadly. My soul had crumbled into shards and nothing else in my body worked properly. I had no hope for anything. All I had was the bottle.

She didn't look at me as she walked out, unable to give me a real goodbye. She shut the door with her back to me. The door clicked when it was shut. Her feet sounded a moment later as she walked down the hallway.

Instead of going after her, I just stood there. I listened to her walk out of my life, taking every joy with her. My life had been ruined and I was doomed forever. I would never find happiness because I wasn't meant to.

I would always be alone.

***

After an endless night of drinking, I knew I couldn't give up. My life would be a bitter and sad story unless I did something to fix this. I would do whatever it took. I was a good man, and I deserved the woman I loved.

No one was taking her away from me.

I wasn't sure if Sara still lived in the same apartment, but I had to give it a try. If not, I'd have to do some digging until I figured out exactly where she went. But fortunately, I found the right place.

Sara opened the door to my cold expression. She flinched slightly when she saw me, afraid of me.

I hated looking at her. I hated those stupid green eyes and that blonde hair. I hated the fact I asked her out to begin with. I should have just kept going and found a nice girl somewhere else. Instead, I slept with the devil. "Can I have a moment of your time?" My jaw was clenched tightly, and I spoke like a monster. It even scared me a little bit.

"Uh…"

I barged in without being invited and sat on her couch. Her apartment was exactly as I remembered it. We had sex on that couch a few times. And on the floor. And on the coffee table.

Repulsive.

Sara slowly followed me into the living room and sat on the other couch. She stared at me in surprise, unable to believe I was really there—in her living room. She kept her legs pressed tightly together and her hands in her lap. "What can I help you with?"

I stared at her TV because I didn't want to look at her. I hated her face. It wasn't the past that bothered me. It wasn't the fact she cheated on me. I got over that. It was the fact she was ruining the greatest thing that ever happened to me. "I saw you with Leo at Tito's. You were making out with him against the bar. I watched you for two minutes before I walked out."

She held my gaze, and slowly her face paled and became translucent. It was the same color as snow and just as icy. Her green eyes dimmed when she'd been cornered, and as much as she tried to hide her fear, she couldn't.

"I didn't confront you because I was so hurt. I just left the jewelry store because I bought you a fucking engagement ring, and then I see you making out with your ex. I was in so much shock I didn't know what to do. So I left."

Her breathing picked up. Her chest rose and fell with heavy pants. A million thoughts swirled in her eyes. She couldn't hide the panic exploding through her. She was deteriorating by the second.

"I never told you because I wanted you to suffer. I wanted you to wonder why I left. I wanted you to be paranoid, to worry if I figured out what you were doing when you claimed to be at work. I wanted my absence to haunt you. And I think I succeeded."

She finally looked away, unable to hold my gaze any longer.

"So stop lying to Taylor, and tell her the truth."

There was no reaction. She purposely looked away.

"Tell her."

"I'm not telling her anything..."

My skin prickled with unease. The threat was in the air. "Excuse me?"

"I already told her I didn't cheat on you." Her voice was weak despite her defiance. She reminded me of a child, scared of discipline.

"Then retract your statement."

"I can't do that."

"Why the fuck not?"

"Because...I can't handle the two of you being together. It will jeopardize my friendship with Taylor, and I don't want to see your face all the time."

"Too damn bad. Maybe you shouldn't have cheated on me."

She turned back to me, the fire in her eyes. "How do you think I've felt for the past two years? I kept going over our relationship in my head, trying to figure out exactly what went wrong. I wondered if it was something I did or said. I wondered if I pushed you away somewhere. It was torture."

"Good." I didn't feel bad—at all.

"What you did to me was way worse than what I did to you."

"Oh, really?" I snapped. "Because what you did to me cost me ten thousand dollars."

She raised an eyebrow.

"Your ring. I couldn't take it back so I gave it to a bum. And you wasted a year of my life. I was so fucked up after what you did to me that I got lost. I lived my life by the bottle and by the women who slept in my bed. And then Taylor came in and changed my life completely. She fixed me. You don't get to break my heart once and then do it again by taking her away from me."

She held her silence.

"I'm a nice guy, so I'm going to give you an offer. If you really don't want her to know you lied, tell her you're okay with the two of us being together, that you want your best friend to be happy. You know, like all friends should be. I won't tell her what we talked about, and we can forget the whole thing."

She looked away again. "No."

"No?" I hissed.

"You ruined me for two years. I'm not helping you."

This bitch had a lot of nerve.

"You told Leo, didn't you?" she whispered. "Because he left me the same day."

I was surprised she pieced the puzzle together. "Yep. I told him." I went to him the day after I caught them together. Instead of punching him in the face like I should have, I informed him Sara was two-timing both of us. He didn't know I existed, and he was just as pissed off for being played. We agreed not to tell her what we knew. We just dumped her. "And I don't feel bad about it. Maybe you should open your legs for one guy at a time."

She didn't react to the insult even though I knew she was pissed. "I'm not telling her anything. Payback is a bitch, ain't it?"

"You're psycho, you know that?" How did I not realize how much of a freak she was? How did I fall in love with this insane person? "You were the one who started everything by cheating on me. I had every right to do what I did."

"No. You were spiteful."

"And what are you doing now?"

She crossed her arms over her chest.

"This is the bottom line. You're hurting Taylor, the innocent person in all of this. She loves me and wants to be with me. How can you stand in the way of that? How can you hurt someone you claim to love?"

"I feel bad for hurting her. But she shouldn't be dating you at all. It's still a conflict of interest."

"But this is entirely your fault. You were the one who snuck around."

"It shouldn't matter," she whispered. "I'm not letting you get what you want, not after what you did to me."

I couldn't believe what I was hearing. Her need for revenge was so twisted it was insane. One day, she would be locked up for murder, I was sure of it. The fact Taylor trusted her so much was even more depressing. "Sara, I'm proposing to Taylor. I already have a ring. As soon as she's finished moving in, I'm getting down on one knee. And I know she'll say yes."

Her face contorted into a look of anger.

"Don't take away the happiest day of your best friend's life. It's not right."

She refused to look at me.

"Seriously?" I asked in shock. "You're still going to lie to her? What happens when I tell her what we talked about?"

"I'll deny it. And she'll believe me."

Wow. "You're sick, you know that?"

"Maybe," she whispered. "But it looks like you're single."

Chapter Sixteen

Taylor

It was late in the evening when a knock sounded on my door.

The only person who would visit me right now was Volt. I finally stopped crying an hour ago, and the puffiness in my eyes hadn't quite died down. I fixed my face as much as possible before I opened the door.

He walked inside, angry. His shoulders were tense like he was prepared for a battle. His eyes were darker than they'd ever been before.

"Everything okay?"

"I talked to Sara."

The last thing I expected him to do was go to her. I wasn't even sure what a conversation between them would be like. Until that point, I'd never seen them utter a word to each other.

"I confronted her about the whole thing. She admitted to it."

"She did?" I asked in surprise.

He nodded. "I told her I spotted her with Leo. I told her I later told Leo she was playing both of us, which was why he dumped her the same day I did. And I told her not to lie to you."

Would Sara really lie to me? I couldn't believe it. "But I just asked her."

"She doesn't want you to be with me, and she's willing to lie to make that happen. She's angry at me for hurting her. She's angry with me for playing her so well."

"But…" I still couldn't wrap my head around it. "I need to ask her myself."

"Isn't my word good enough?" He asked. "I was just there. I just told you everything that happened."

"She's my best friend, Volt. I want to hear it from her mouth."

He growled in frustration. "If you go over there, she's just going to lie to you. That's what I'm telling you. Why isn't my word good enough for you? She's playing us both."

"Your word is good enough for me," I argued. "But I want to confront her myself. I'll tell her you told me everything. How will she be able to get out of that?"

He shook his head in anger. "Taylor, why don't you believe me?"

"I never said I didn't believe you."

"You think I'm making all of this up?"

"I didn't say that either."

"Then accept my story and accept the fact your friend is a lying psychopath."

I couldn't accept that part. "Just let me talk to her."

He crossed his arms over his chest. "She's just going to lie to you."

"I have to give her the benefit of the doubt."

"The only way it's possible she didn't lie is if I made up this entire story. You really think I would do that? If you actually believe that, then why were we ever together at all?"

"Volt, that's not what I said," I snapped. "Just calm down."

"I'm not going to fucking calm down. I've been telling the truth this entire time, but you keep siding with that stupid cunt—"

"Don't call her—"

"I'll call her whatever the fuck I want." He took a step forward, making me back up in fear. "I'll never understand why you trust her so much. She's a lying whore. You should believe me. I'm your best friend. I've never lied to you."

"She's never lied to me either. Just let me talk to her." We'd been friends forever. Not once in that time span had she ever lied to me. This situation was complex and didn't make any sense. The only way to get to the bottom of it was by interviewing both sides. "I'm not saying you're lying. I'm not saying she's lying. Just let me talk to both parties so I can figure out what happened."

He stepped back from me, about to snap. He needed to put space between us so I wouldn't get in the crossfire. "Fine. Whatever. Talk to her. But don't expect me to wait around for the verdict." He stormed out of my apartment without shutting the door behind him. I heard his heavy footfalls as he walked out, his anger echoing in the hallway.

I grabbed my purse and keys and prepared to pay a visit to Sara. All my drive disappeared in that moment. Just a short while ago, I was happy. I had everything I needed. But now it seemed like a lifetime ago, something I would never see again.

***

I walked into Sara's apartment, and everything felt exactly the same.

"Hey, what's up?" She was in her pajamas with her hair in a bun. "I was about to head to bed. Everything alright?"

If she just had a conversation with Volt, it didn't seem like it. The TV was on, and she was watching her favorite reality TV show. A bottle of wine sat there, like usual. "Uh, Volt just came by my place and said he stopped by?"

"Yeah, he did. He was only here for five minutes then he left."

"And what happened?" I didn't make any assumptions because that would be wrong. She'd been my best friend forever. I was sure she had an explanation for what happened. And if she did cheat on Volt and lied about it beforehand, she would come clean now. I had faith.

"He said I cheated on him. Said he saw me in a bar with some guy. I told him that wasn't me. He probably saw a woman who looked just like me. But it wasn't me."

"Oh...what did he say?"

"He kept repeating the same story, saying it was me. But I knew where I was that night. I was working late because I fell behind on one of the projects. I told him I would find my time card and show it to him, but he didn't want to hear about it. He's so fixated that I cheated on him that he won't listen to any other explanation."

"Because he said you admitted it…" I was getting two completely different stories.

Someone was lying.

Who was it?

"No, he misunderstood me." She sat on the couch and grabbed her glass of wine. "I said I understood why he assumed it was me. I mean, there are blondes everywhere. And I also understood why he left me, even if it wasn't the right thing to do. But I never said I cheated on him—because I didn't."

Maybe it was just a misunderstanding. Volt had a bad temper sometimes and maybe he was so frustrated by our situation he didn't listen correctly. Maybe he just listened for things he wanted to hear and tuned everything else out. He didn't lie to me. He just shared his side of the story. "Sorry to bother you this late at night. I just wanted to get the full story."

"I feel bad for him," she whispered. "He's trying so hard to make this work. I'm sure he's willing to lie about it. I mean, it's obvious how much he loves you. I can't blame him for working so hard."

I knew Volt wanted to make this work, but I doubted he would lie to make it happen. Misleading people wasn't in his nature. Never had been. But when times were desperate, people did desperate things. "Well, thanks for talking to me."

"No problem. Don't be too hard on him. He's a good guy."

When she was sweet and caring, how could I believe she would ever lie? It must have just been a huge misunderstanding. "I know he is."

***

After work the next day, I called him.

He picked up but didn't speak into the phone.

"Volt?"

"What?"

I ignored his hostility. "Can I come by? I talked to Sara."

"No. I don't have time for this."

"Time for what?"

"You believe her."

"I never said that. Can I come by so we can talk about it? I'd rather not have this conversation on the phone." I was walking down the sidewalk with people passing me. Voices carried to my ear, making it difficult to concentrate on what he was saying.

"Whatever." He hung up.

I sighed and shoved the phone into my pocket, knowing this conversation would be difficult. He was so upset he couldn't see reason. I didn't blame him. I'd been there before.

I walked inside his apartment and saw him standing in the entryway, waiting for me.

"What?" he barked. "Get this shit over with."

I set my bag down. "Why are you being a dick right now?"

"Because you believe her. It's bullshit."

"I never said that."

"What else did you come here to say? If you believed me, you would've had a very different reaction over the phone." He crossed his arms over his chest, his facial hair coming in from not shaving for a few days.

"I talked to her last night, and I think I know what happened."

"Oh, really?" His voice was full of condescension. "Enlighten me."

"She said she never cheated on you, but you still think she did. She even has an alibi, but you still didn't believe her. It sounds like a misunderstanding on both parts."

Out of nowhere, he started laughing, high and maniacal. The piercing sound filled the apartment, hurting my ears because it was so loud. "Fuck, you're stupid." He kept laughing. "This is just...it's so stupid it's funny."

I narrowed my eyes, the insult hurting. "Excuse me?"

"I said you're fucking stupid." He stopped laughing, giving me the coldest stare I'd ever seen. "I'm done with us, Taylor. I'm officially finished. I don't want to work on this relationship. I don't want to be with you." He opened a drawer in his kitchen and pulled out a small device. It looked like a recorder. Along with it was a small, black box. It looked like a jewelry case. "I don't want a woman who doesn't trust me. I don't want a woman who doesn't believe a word I say." He grabbed the recorder and set it on the kitchen table beside me. "I knew Sara was a lying cunt. So when I went over there, I recorded the entire conversation. I was afraid this would happen. I was afraid you'd pick her over me. And you know what? You did." He peered into my face, nothing but hatred residing deep inside. "Listen to it.

289

Then get the fuck out of my apartment." He slammed his fist down on the table, making a sound so loud it made me jolt. He walked to the door. "Goodbye, Taylor. Hope you and Sara are very happy together."

***

"Sara, I'm proposing to Taylor. I already have a ring. As soon as she's finished moving in, I'm getting down on one knee. And I know she'll say yes."

Sara didn't respond. There was just a pause.

"Don't take away the happiest day of your best friend's life. It's not right."

Sara still didn't speak.

"Seriously?" Volt asked in shock. "You're still going to lie to her? What happens when I tell her what we talked about?"

"I'll deny it. And she'll believe me."

Oh. My. God.

Volt's voice was full of hatred. "You're sick, you know that?"

"Maybe," she whispered. "But it looks like you're single."

The recorder ended and went silent.

I stared at it and waited for something else to happen. But nothing ever did. I looked at the box Volt left behind. Inside was the ring he bought for me, the ring I would never wear.

I couldn't process what just happened. I wasn't sure if I was more depressed that Volt left me or that Sara lied to my face—twice. She didn't care about my happiness. All she cared about was herself.

I felt stupid.

I sacrificed my relationship with Volt just to give her the benefit of the doubt. I wanted to do the right thing by being pragmatic. I knew there was an explanation that showed them both in a good light.

But I was wrong.

Very wrong.

I fell into the chair and tried not to give into the grief. I didn't just lose Volt. I lost Sara too. She was my best friend, my family. And she stabbed me so hard in the back I couldn't breathe.

Now what did I do?

I lost everything that mattered to me. The happy life I had once before disappeared like a puff of smoke.

Everything I believed in had been shaken. Volt turned his back on me, and I knew I couldn't blame him for it.

I stared the box and felt my fingers tingle. I wanted to open it, to look inside and see he had picked out for me. As soon as I finished moving in, he was going to ask me to spend his life with him.

And I would have said yes.

I couldn't open the lid. If I saw the ring, it would just make this a million times harder. If I saw the special diamond he picked out just for me, the ring he imagined me wearing until we were old and gray, I would collapse then and there.

I had to keep going.

I left the kitchen table, leaving the recorder and the ring behind. This was the last time I would ever be in Volt's apartment, so I gathered my things before I walked out. I didn't want to come back there again. I didn't want to look at him. If I did, I would just break down.

I got my stuff and left.

***

Sara opened the door, sweaty and in her gym clothes. She must have just got home. "Hey, I—"

"I can't believe you lied to me." Now that I was face-to-face with her, I couldn't control my rage. I never wanted to hit someone before, but I desperately wanted to slap her hard across the face.

Shit, I wanted to bitch slap her.

She kept up her charade. "Taylor, I didn't lie about anything. Volt is the one—"

"I'm this close to knocking your teeth out." I pushed her back, making her stumble until she got her footing again. "Volt recorded the conversation the two of you had. I heard everything you said. And don't make up some bullshit about it being fabricated because I recognized your voice, and I heard Desperate Housewives in the background."

Sara's face immediately changed. Her innocent charade disappeared once she'd been caught.

And somehow that made things worse. "I can't believe you did this to me."

"Taylor, let me explain—"

"You don't need to. I heard the recording. All you cared about was getting back at him for what he did to you. You were willing to sacrifice my happiness to make it happen." I placed my hand across my chest. "Your best friend. What's wrong with you?"

"I..." She struggled to find an explanation but couldn't. "I don't know. I just... I didn't want you to know I did that. You would think less of me."

"I would never think less of you for anything— besides lying. So yes, I think you're scum now."

Her eyes flinched in pain.

"And the fact you would hurt me like that, turn me against Volt because you knew I blindly trusted you...makes me sick."

She dropped her face, shame in her eyes.

"Volt is gone. He left me."

She didn't move.

"He left me because I didn't believe him. I insisted on giving you the benefit of the doubt, knowing there was some other explanation for what happened. He got fed up with me and left. He gave me the ring and walked out. I can't go after him and try to make our relationship work because I don't blame him for leaving. I'd judge him if he stayed. And that's all your fault." I poked her hard in the chest. I was so angry, tears formed in my eyes. I was frustrated for being punished for trying to do the right thing. I refused to choose my boyfriend over my best friend, and I refused to choose my best friend over my boyfriend. But I still got screwed in the end. "I'll never forgive you for this, Sara. I can't even look at you." I was done with this friendship—or whatever the hell it was. Was any of it ever real? Did it ever mean anything? "Don't contact me. I mean it." I walked out of her apartment for the last time and shut the door.

Once I was down the hallway, I felt the tears of sorrow drip down my face. I hated her so much for what she did to me, but I was still saying goodbye to a piece of myself. Sara was family to me, and now she was gone. I broke up with the two people I loved most in the same day.

It was a miracle I was still standing.

***

Volt never called me. And I didn't expect him to.

I unpacked everything back in my apartment and tossed the boxes in the trash. It looked just the way it did before I left, but it would never feel quite the same. It was where I lived now, but Volt's place was still home in my heart.

Going through his things and hiding them away was the hardest part. I knew he wasn't coming back. From now on, I would sleep in my bed alone. One day, I would be well enough to start dating again, and a new man would sleep beside me. But the thought of that happening brought me even more sorrow.

I really had to move on without him.

I was grateful it wasn't summertime yet, and the kids were still in school. If I didn't have work to focus on, the depression would swallow me whole. I did my best to concentrate on my students and give them the best education possible. They were actually helping me more than they realized. It was a safe place away from home, a place where I didn't think about the man who left me.

The gang didn't contact me or ask me questions about our breakup. They either knew and understood I needed space. Or they didn't have a clue and would know soon enough.

I didn't want to talk about it.

Sara didn't call me either. She was smart enough not to reach out to me. If she did, I might actually slap her. My fondness for her slowly faded and hatred took over completely. I couldn't believe I trusted someone so blindly. And then she backstabbed me the second I got in her way.

Was anyone trustworthy?

Volt immediately came into my mind. He was always loyal to me, right from the beginning.

But I screwed that up.

Over the span of two weeks, I lost a lot of weight. I wasn't sure how it was possible since I didn't exercise. But I didn't eat anything so it made sense. When I felt like I would pass out, I ate crackers because that was all I could handle.

Every day seemed to pass slower than the last. Sometimes I wondered what Volt was doing, but I knew it was best not to think about it. He'd probably already had a few girls over, occupying the bed I once slept in.

When the thoughts made me cry, I forced myself to stop.

I had to move on.

I had to keep going.

Maybe, one day, if I were lucky enough, I would be happy again.

Or maybe not.

Chapter Seventeen

Volt

"Holy shit." Derek stared at me with wide eyes. "I can't believe that."

"Well, believe it." I downed the shot then told the bartender to pour me another.

She came over to me, her boobalicious chest on display for everyone to see. "Wow. You're a drinker, aren't you?"

"I sure am, sweetheart." I tapped my glass on the counter.

She filled it to the brim before she gave me a smile.

I winked.

She walked away and tended to the other customers. Before her shift was over, she'd probably give me her number.

And I'd take it.

Derek grabbed my shoulder. "What the hell? It's really over?"

"Yeah." I clanked my glass against his. "I'm single again. It's great."

He stared at me incredulously. "Are you high?"

"High on life, maybe."

"Volt, give Taylor another chance. You're being unfair."

"I'm being unfair?" I asked incredulously. "I told her what happened and she didn't believe me—twice."

"She never said that. She said she just wanted to get the whole story."

"But she still dumped me—twice."

"It was a complicated situation. Cut her some slack."

"No." I would never give her any slack. I gave that woman my heart, my body, my soul. And she didn't give me anything. When it mattered most, she wasn't there for me.

"Volt—"

"No." I made my decision, and I was sticking with it. "It's done."

Derek stared at me with a sad expression. "I know you love her."

"Loved her. Past tense."

"Love doesn't die overnight."

"It did for me." I downed the glass and needed another.

"I don't believe you. Just talk to her."

"She hasn't tried talking to me. She's given up."

"Or maybe she knows you don't want to see her."

"Whatever. It doesn't matter." I waved the bartender over and ordered another round.

She happily obliged and poured the liquor. "I get off in an hour. You want to hang out?"

"Absolutely." I had to get back on the horse, pronto.

Derek stared at me with disapproval. "I can't watch this."

"Watch what?"

He slid off the barstool. "Watch you throw your life away."

***

Penny and I left the bar and headed to my place.

"Wow." She squeezed close to my side. "You have a place by Park Avenue?"

"Yep."

"Ooh...I can't wait to see your apartment."

I was getting laid. I knew it. "I think you'll like my bedroom especially."

"I'm sure I will." She tucked her arm through mine.

We arrived at my building, and the second I looked at it, I suddenly felt ill. That apartment reeked of Taylor. Her spirit was ingrained in the walls, the floor, everything.

And I immediately felt like I was doing something wrong.

"What's up?" she asked, wondering why we stopped.

I had every right to do this but something was holding me back. "I just realized I have somewhere to be. I'm sorry." I didn't look at her as I said it, feeling guilty for flirting with her to begin with.

"Uh...okay. Everything alright?"

No. Nothing was all right. "I'm sorry. It was nice meeting you." I pulled out of her grasp and walked away, heading right past my building. I kept going even though I had nowhere to be.

I shoved my hands in my pockets and felt the liquor burn me from the inside out. It was easier to be drunk because it chased away the pain. But now it just amplified my feelings. I felt so alone.

I felt dead inside.

When I looked up, I realized I was at the orphanage. My feet naturally carried me there. I didn't even realize where I was going until I arrived. I looked at the second story window and saw Clay.

He was sitting in the nook where I last saw him. He peered out the window like a bird in a cage, desperate to be free. He played with his pocket knife, trailing it across his palm slowly.

Looking at him gave me comfort. Just being close to him made me feel alive again. It gave me purpose. It gave me...something. I stood there on the abandoned sidewalk and wondered if he would notice me.

Clay put his pocketknife away and prepared to leave the windowsill. He was either going to bed or finding some other activity to do. By a stroke of luck, he looked out the window.

And saw me.

I stood with my hands in my pockets, the cold surrounding me. The frost was even worse in the evening, and I could feel my knuckles crack from the dryness. But the pain was welcomed. Because all I felt was pain.

Our eyes locked, and I stared at the face that brought me joy. I stared at the face I loved.

His eyes were stoic as he looked at me, neither happiness nor hatred there.

I felt my eyes water just from looking at him. I felt my body give into the turmoil of grief. I felt sick—deathly ill. Clay still hated me and would always hate me. He would turn around at any moment and never look at me again.

But he didn't.

He sat back on the windowsill and looked at me. The usual hatred in his eyes disappeared and concern replaced it. He watched me for a long time, understanding I was suffering. I was dying. I was fighting just to breathe. He did something I never expected and pressed his palm against the window.

My chest automatically sucked in a deep breath, taking comfort in the gesture. Despite what I'd done, he was still there for me when I was at my lowest point. He still cared about me when it mattered.

He still loved me.

***

I filled out all the necessary paperwork and met with the director of the orphanage. After a long conversation about my income, my household atmosphere, my drug test, and every other invasive procedure you could think of, I finally got approved.

I filled out the final signatures before I passed the papers back to Mathilda, one of the sisters who looked after the kids.

"Mr. Rosenthal, there's one last step of the procedure."

"What is it?"

"A child can only be adopted by consent. If he doesn't want to go with you, he doesn't have to."

"I understand."

"Then go talk to him and see how he feels."

This was the scary part. If he said no, I would die inside. All hope I had left would be gone. "Thank you." I walked into the back room where the kids hung out. There weren't as many today, probably because they were in their dorms or they were still at school.

Clay was in his usual spot. He looked exactly the same with the exception of his hair. It was short because he just got a haircut. I walked over to him and pulled up a chair.

He looked at me the way he did the other night when he spotted me outside. He searched my gaze and found my agony. No vicious comments left his mouth today. "Are you okay?"

"No." That was the honest truth. I wouldn't lie to him.

"What happened?"

"I left Taylor—for good."

"Oh. Why?"

It was a long and boring story. "Nothing worth mentioning."

He pulled his knees to his chest. "You seem pretty down."

"I'm a bit lost. I'll admit it."

"Is there anything I can do?" He was being nice to me when I didn't deserve it.

"No. But there's something I want to ask you."

"What?" He put his pocketknife away. "I haven't started on my college applications yet. Just haven't had the chance."

"We'll get to that soon. Don't worry."

He stared at me in silence, having no idea what I was going to say.

"Clay, I met with the director and filled out all the necessary paperwork. I've signed everything. I'm legally able to take you home with me—if you want to come."

His eyes widened but his face didn't react in any other way. He couldn't hide his shock over what he just heard. "What...what do you mean?"

"I want to adopt you."

"You're serious?"

"Absolutely. You're my family, Clay. We may not be related by blood, but that doesn't matter. Water is thicker than blood sometimes."

"You...you want me to live with you?"

I nodded. "If you want to come with me. You have a choice. You don't have to do it if you don't want to."

"No, I do," he said quickly. "I just...didn't expect you to do this."

"I should have done it a long time ago. I think about you every day. I always worry about you. I miss you... I love you." Maybe I wasn't ready to be a parent, but I was ready to be a guardian. This kid had changed my life in so many good ways. He should be home with me. He should be under my roof.

"I...I don't know what to say."

"You don't have to answer me right now. Take some time to think about it."

"No, I want to come," he said. "I just want...to make sure that's what you want."

There wasn't a doubt in my mind. My house wasn't a home without him. He would do better under my roof, succeed in ways he wouldn't otherwise. And he was a part of my family anyway. "Absolutely."

He scooted to the edge, his limbs shaking with excitement. "I totally want to live with you. Can we go now? Do we have to wait? Should I get my stuff now? Get me out of here, Volt. I hate it here."

I chuckled. "Yes, you can come with me now. But there's one thing we need to talk about."

"What?" Now he was anxious, ready to leave and settle into his new place.

"I'm not your father, and I'm not trying to be. But I am your guardian. That means you need to listen to me. That means you need to obey. We can be friends, but I'm not your friend all the time. Do you understand?"

He nodded. "I get it."

"Alright. Now go get your things."

He jumped off the couch and sprinted across the room, drawing the attention of all the other kids. His feet pounded against the hardwood floor as he took off at full speed. "I'm getting the hell out of here!"

I laughed to myself and waited, happier than I'd been in weeks.

***

Clay took the spare bedroom and kept his space clean. Without me having to tell him, he took care of his laundry, made his bed every morning, and when he used the dishes, he washed them and placed them in the dishwasher.

I was impressed.

When he came home from school, he worked on his homework at the kitchen table, where I usually helped him as we had dinner together. Adopting him was exactly as I pictured it would be, and I wished I'd done it sooner. He was happy.

And I was happy.

At least as happy as I could be at the moment.

My parents kept blowing up my phone and asking what was going on with Taylor. I was supposed to propose a few weeks ago, and obviously, I never did. Her parents wondered what happened to. I'd deflected their questions long enough. Now there was no way to avoid them.

Clay and I went to my parents place for dinner one evening. They didn't know he was coming. They didn't even know I adopted him yet. Tonight would definitely be an interesting evening.

Mom immediately bombarded me with questions the second she opened the door. "Volt, what's going with Taylor? Have you asked her? What happened?"

I was dreading this conversation, but I had to get it over with. "I'll tell you everything when we sit down. And it's cool that I brought Clay along?"

Mom looked at him in surprise. "Of course. Of course."

We walked inside, and I greeted my father. He was friendly with Clay like he was at Thanksgiving. They were both fond of him. Adopting him would probably make them happy—at least I hoped.

"Clay, can you wash your hands before dinner? I need to talk to my parents in private."

"Okay." He didn't give me any attitude and walked off. Now that he lived under my roof, he obeyed me just like I asked. I was surprised by how easy it was. I could only assume he was afraid I would take him back to the orphanage if he was too much trouble.

Which was ridiculous.

Mom immediately asked about Taylor again. "Volt, what the hell is going on? We've been so worried."

"First of all, Taylor and I broke up." Saying her name was still painful. I couldn't sleep without her. I spent most of my time thinking about her, hoping she was doing okay.

She didn't take the ring with her, and now it was sitting in my nightstand. I didn't have the strength to throw it away.

"What?" Mom shrieked. "Why?"

I told her the story about Sara. It was quite a tale, and I probably wouldn't have believed it unless I'd seen it myself.

"Wow," Dad said. "That's insane."

"I know," I said. "We just couldn't work things out." I left out the part where Taylor didn't believe me. I knew that made her look really bad. I had no reason to protect her, but I still felt obligated to. "And...I adopted Clay."

Now Mom was even more shocked. "You did what?"

"Honey, keep your voice down." Dad eyed the hallway, hoping Clay didn't hear Mom's outburst.

"I adopted him last week," I explained. "He lives with me now. Things have been good."

"Volt, adopting a child is a big deal," Mom said. "It's not something you should take lightly."

"I know," I said calmly. "And I never did. I really thought about it before I made this decision."

"You should have consulted with us," Dad said. "You have no experience being a parent."

"Well, thanks," I said sarcastically. "But I'm a grown man, and I can make my own decisions."

"Volt," Mom said fiercely. "You just did this because you're depressed over Taylor. You're trying to fill the hole she left behind. And that's not fair to Clay."

I admit I was depressed about Taylor. Every day was a struggle just to get by. But that wasn't the reason why I brought him into my home. "I adopted him because he's family. And he should be living with family. That orphanage is not a place for him to learn and grow. I can give him a lot more."

"That's very sweet of you," Mom said. "You have a big heart. But this is a huge responsibility. I don't think it was a good idea."

"I love you, Mom. And I don't mean this in a disrespectful way. But, I don't care what you think. Everything has been said and done. He's staying with me and that's final. He's officially your grandson, and I hope you start treating him that way."

Mom and Dad looked at each other, and a silent conversation passed between them. Her eyes softened and his did a moment later. They turned back to me with warmer expressions, understanding it would be pointless to fight me on this.

"We'll love him like our own," Dad said.

"Of course we will," Mom said. "He's a very sweet boy."

"Thank you." That meant a lot to me. I didn't want Clay to be treated as an outsider to this family. He was like a son to me, and I wouldn't tolerate anyone treating him otherwise.

Clay returned to the room. We went shopping the other day, and now he had nice jeans and a long sleeve shirt that actually fit him. When he cleaned up, he actually looked like a handsome boy.

"Volt told us the good news," Mom said. "We're so happy to have you in our family." Mom hugged him tightly, giving him a fierce bear hug like how she gave me. Dad hugged him next, giving him fatherly love right from the start.

"Thanks," Clay said. "Volt is a really great guy. I know how lucky I am."

I smiled at him then wrapped my arm around his shoulders. "We're the lucky ones, kid."

***

We watched TV on the couch together later that night before bed. Clay had a bowl of popcorn in his lap, and he tossed a kernel into the air, catching it in his open mouth. "Booyah."

"I'm impressed," I said sarcastically.

"This shit is hard."

I glared at him.

"Sorry...no cussing."

I turned back to the TV.

"So...what happened with Taylor?" He stopped tossing the popcorn into the air and placed piece-by-piece into his mouth. He kept his voice quiet, like that would lure me to answer.

"She and I just didn't work."

"Why don't you just answer me?" he asked. "I'm almost an adult. I can handle whatever you're going to say."

He wouldn't stop asking questions until I answered. And he had the right to know. She was a part of his life at one time. "Basically, I tried telling her something, and she wouldn't believe me. She took someone else's word over mine. When I proved I was right, it was too late. I was so angry, I didn't want to be with her anymore."

"Why didn't she believe you?"

314

"Her best friend was telling her side of the story. She didn't know who to believe."

"You broke up with her over that?" he asked incredulously.

"It was worse than I made it sound."

He kept eating the bowl of popcorn, the kernels cracking and popping in his mouth. "I liked Taylor."

"Yeah...I did too."

"I miss her."

That just made me miss her more. "We'll be okay, Clay."

"I don't know. I'll never forget the way you looked at me through that window. You looked like you lost everything."

I remembered that night. It was just like all the others—impossible to get through.

"Can I say something?"

"If I say no, you're just going to tell me anyway."

"I think you're being too hard on her. It's okay to be mad...but to break up with her is a little harsh."

"How so?" Why was I listening to the opinion of a teenager?

"Well…I was really pissed at you for contacting social services. It was a betrayal. I trusted you not to do it, and you did it anyway. It really hurt…but I understood why you did it. In time, I knew I was being unfair. I knew you were in a difficult situation and had no other choice."

I turned his way, touched by what he said.

"It sounds similar. You're hurt because she betrayed you, but you understand why she did. Maybe you should cut her some slack. I mean, if you love her, there should be no reason not to be with her."

His words sank into me heavily. They embedded in my skin and reached my heart. A kid who knew nothing about love just gave me a lesson in forgiveness.

"Just don't wait too long. You don't want to miss your chance."

Chapter Eighteen

Taylor

After another god-awful day, I just wanted to go home and sit in my apartment. I wanted to be alone even though I was constantly alone. My apartment still held Volt's presence, and sometimes, that comforted me.

Sometimes, it broke me.

My students forced me to put on a good smile and be whatever they needed me to be. But without that support, I fell back into a lonely person. My shoulders slacked, and I didn't care about anything. I hadn't gone grocery shopping in weeks, but I was so depressed that I didn't care.

I didn't care about anything.

I wanted to call Volt just to hear his voice. I wanted to talk like we used to, even if it didn't go anywhere. If we just talked about the weather, I would be okay with that. Not talking to my best friend every day was dreadful. The fact I would never talk to him again was just more painful.

When I arrived at my door, someone was standing in front of it. With bright blonde hair and remorseful eyes, she looked at me with pure desperation. It reeked from her clothes.

Just looking at her pissed me off. I used to find comfort in her smile. Now I just loathed her, hated her. There was no chance of forgiveness. My heart was too black, too cold, for that. "Get the fuck away from me." The profanity flew from my mouth like it was the most natural thing in the world.

Sara cowered like I slapped her across the face. "I know you hate me right now—"

"No. I hate you all the time." I pushed her aside so I could unlock my door.

"Taylor, I'm so sorry. Please, just give me five minutes to tell you how sorry I am."

"I'll pass." I swung the door open and marched inside.

"Taylor, come on. I hate myself for what I did—"

I kicked the door shut and locked it.

She didn't knock on the door or turn the knob. She went quiet, accepting my dismissal.

I set my things down and immediately went into the shower. The hot running water acted as a cocoon for my wounds. It wrapped me up tightly and kept me afloat. The sound blocked out most of my thoughts. When I cried, I couldn't hear myself because everything was muffled.

This was my life now. Crying in the shower.

This is what it'd come to.

I had to start over. I had to stand on my feet and move on. I had to forget about the perfect life I threw away and continue forward. In theory, it sounded plausible. But in reality, it seemed impossible.

All I could do was sit there—and cry.

Chapter Nineteen

Volt

When I was alone, my thoughts swallowed me whole.

There was no escape from the pain in my heart. Taylor's face came into my mind's eyes, her beautiful brown hair contrasting against those bright, blue eyes. Her lips were full and curved like a bow. I remembered every detail because they was impossible to forget.

I missed her.

My anger was still prevalent, building inside me with bitterness. But sometimes, it would disappear altogether, and I would be left with longing. I would be left empty.

Taylor hadn't contacted me. I expected her to come by the apartment or at least send me a text. But she never did. When I left that ring there, she knew I meant business. She knew I would never ask her to marry me after the shit she put me through. She knew she was wrong when she listened to Sara. She knew she was wrong for doubting me.

But I still expected her to fight.

A part of me was disappointed when she didn't.

And the other part was just relieved.

When Clay first moved in with me, my natural instinct was to call her and tell her what I'd done. I wanted her support. I wanted her to tell me I could handle raising a teenager with no experience. I needed to know I did the right thing.

But now I would never find out.

I was sitting at my desk in my office when my secretary informed me I had a visitor. My first instinct was Taylor. Maybe she came to talk to me, cornering me in my office so I couldn't simply run away.

My heart pounded.

Excitement rushed through me.

I was suddenly out of breath.

I told my secretary to send her in, remaining calm and collective. A poker face was important. Since nothing had changed in our relationship, I couldn't give her any hint of hope. I had to remain strong—indifferent.

The door opened, but Taylor didn't walk inside.

It was Sara.

My mood evaporated like a wisp of smoke. I wanted to grab my desk and throw it at her. I hated this woman— loathed her. Somehow, I hated her even more every time I looked at her.

I despised her.

"Get the fuck out." I pointed at the door, refusing to give her a chance to speak. She had nothing important to say to me. Even if she did, I refused to hear it. "Now. Or I'll call security and have them throw you out."

She hovered near the door, afraid to come any closer to me.

"Go," I barked.

"Just give me five minutes. Please."

"I don't owe you a goddamn thing."

"It's about Taylor." She found the strength to take a step forward, coming closer to my circle. If she crept too close, I could snatch her and carry her out. "Just listen to me, okay?"

When she mentioned Taylor's name, my body immediately tightened in concern. Maybe this was just a way to bait me, but it worked. "Is she okay?" My voice softened automatically, showing the love that wouldn't die.

"She's...terrible." She came closer to my desk now that my rage had been subdued. "She's devastated."

"But she's not hurt? Not sick?"

"I think so. I've never seen her this low."

So they were still friends? Unbelievable.

"I came here today to beg you to give her another chance. I'm the reason you guys aren't together and that's just wrong. She loves you. You love her. Please, forgive her. It's not her fault."

"She put you up to this?" I asked incredulously.

"No." Her eyes fell. "She won't talk to me..."

At least Taylor learned something.

"She said she never wants to see me again. She hates me." Her bottom lip quivered. "We aren't friends anymore."

"Good riddance," I snapped. "Taylor deserves better."

She stared at the floor for a few seconds before she looked at me again. "Muriel—"

"Don't. Call. Me. That."

She nodded and cleared her throat. "Volt, please give her another chance. I tricked her. I lied to her. I manipulated her. I took advantage of her trusting nature and turned it against her. She didn't do anything wrong. She just wanted to give me the benefit of the doubt..."

"I can't believe you lied to her like that." I shook my head. "If I hadn't recorded it, she never would have figured it out. You're only talking to me because you think if I take her back, you'll be forgiven. You never would have come clean to her. You would have gotten your way, and Taylor would have lost the love of her life anyway. This is entirely selfish. You think you'll be forgiven if you make this right."

She clutched her hands together in front of her waist. "Taylor will never forgive me for what I did. Even if I pull off a miracle and you march over there and propose, she still won't forgive me. It's too late to save myself. What's done is done. I have to live with the consequences forever."

It was the first time I stopped hating her, even if it was just for a second. "I don't understand why you did this in the first place..."

"Honestly, I don't either. I guess I didn't want to lose Taylor. If she married you, I would be tossed to the side. I would be constantly reminded that she got Prince Charming and I'm alone. I just... It didn't work out in my favor."

Questions came to mind that I never asked before. There was never an opportunity to gain this knowledge. But now there was. "Why? Why did you cheat on me? I thought we were happy."

She flinched at the question, not expecting it. "I...I don't know."

"You don't know?" I asked incredulously. "Was I not giving you enough? Was I bad in bed?"

"No, of course not," she whispered. "Leo called me, and we started talking again. Old feelings flared up, and I couldn't tell him about you. And then one thing led to another…it just happened."

I shook my head, disappointed. I was hoping she would have a reason. I was hoping I did something to make her betray me like that. But the fact there was no reason just made things worse. When she told me she loved me, she didn't mean it. When she made love to me, it was just an act. It was depressing.

"Taylor would never do that to you. I heard her talk about you for a year before I realized who you were. Believe me, she's over-the-moon in love with you. She thinks you're the greatest guy on the planet. She's hopelessly and pathetically in love with you. Please give her another chance."

"Why should I?" I asked coldly. "She didn't believe me. If she loved me so much, she should have trusted me more."

"It was a difficult situation. In case you haven't noticed, I'm a good liar. I played you, and I played her... You know how easy it is to be misled."

Yeah, that was certain.

"Volt, please. I know you love her. She loves you." She placed her hands in front of her chest, begging me.

"Why are you doing this?"

"I already told you," she whispered. "I want to make this right for her. It's the least I can do."

"And you want me to talk to her on your behalf?" She must want something. People like her didn't do things for no reason at all.

"No. You don't need to do that. It won't make a difference anyway."

I stared at her and saw the sincerity in her eyes.

"Just think about it. There's no reason strong enough for two people not to be together when they love each other. And love has never been a problem for either of you." She silently excused herself and turned to the door. Her head was bowed, still covered in shame.

I watched her go without saying goodbye. The door clicked shut, and I was alone with my thoughts again. I lowered myself back into the chair and stared at my blank screen. The conversation played back to me in real time. I thought of many things. What should I do? What should I not do? Should I leave things the way they were? Or should I get my ass up and get back the woman I loved?

Chapter Twenty

Taylor

I finally went to the grocery store and picked up a few things. If I didn't eat something substantial soon, I would pass out and never wake up. I grabbed sandwich meat and bread, and a few cans of soup. My muscles had atrophied from doing absolutely nothing for the past few weeks, and I could hardly carry the bags.

I still had my bag from school, and in each arm was a bag from the grocery store. My shoulders screamed from the weight because they lacked any strength. I took the elevator to my floor but even that was difficult.

After the doors opened, I carried everything to my apartment. But the bag was tearing from the cans of soup. If I didn't get there quick enough, it would rip and spill all over the floor. Then I would have to chase them down and carry each one individually.

The bag stretched even more, and I knew I wasn't going to make it. I practically ran to the door, my eyes on the bag. I didn't make it in time and the bag ripped altogether, dropping five cans of soup as they rolled in every direction in front of my apartment. I stared at the ground and watched the carton of milk fall out with it too.

All motivation died within me. It took weeks of preparation just to get me to go to the store in the first place. Now that I accomplished it, everything went to shit. I just didn't care anymore. I screamed to myself then slid to the floor in front of my door. It was a stupid thing to cry over, but that's what I wanted to do. Curl into a ball and just cry.

Footsteps sounded and someone picked up every can. I didn't look up but I watched his shoes. They were black vans, something Volt used to wear once in a while. He grabbed each can then placed them on the floor beside me, next to the bag that was still intact.

"Thanks…" My voice was so quiet he probably didn't hear it.

He sat down beside me, sitting dangerously close for a stranger. "You're welcome."

I recognized that voice. It accompanied my dreams. It was in my fantasies. It was the song I heard in my head when I walked to work. I turned my face slowly, not wanting to get my hopes up. If it was really him, I would cry. Cry harder than I already was.

My eyes locked to his, and I saw the man of my dreams. I saw the man I was still in love with. I saw the man

I threw away. I quickly turned away because my eyes watered. I was a mess, and I was embarrassed to be seen this way. I couldn't even carry groceries because I was so weak.

"Hey." He grabbed my chin and forced my gaze back to his.

Our faces were close together, and his touch was divine. It was the first time I felt good in weeks. It was the first time I could take a full breath without shaking. "Hey."

His fingers rubbed my cheek gently, giving me the kind of affection he used to give me on a daily basis. "I miss you."

Instead of making me feel good, those words only hurt. "This is so hard for me, Volt. I've never been the kind of woman to cry over a man. I've never been the kind of person to give up living when someone walks away. I've never been the damsel in distress. But that's exactly what I am. I'm barely holding on, and I'm not sure if I'll ever recover. If this doesn't mean anything and you're just lonely, please leave. You're making this so much harder on me."

His thumb moved down my cheek until it rested in the corner of my mouth. He gave me a look full of pity before he leaned in and gave me a soft kiss, a kiss full of agony.

Our lips hardly moved together. They just touched— barely.

"I am lonely," he whispered against my mouth. "But I'm also miserable without you. And this does mean something."

I took a deep breath, the kind that actually hurt my ribs. Tears sprouted from my eyes, falling like drops in a waterfall.

He wiped them away with the pads of his thumbs. "I'm so sorry."

"You shouldn't be sorry," I whispered. "It was my fault."

"I'm sorry for leaving. I should have stayed. I should have worked this out with you."

"No, you had every right to be upset. I was the stupid one. I was the idiot who believe everything that stupid cunt said."

Volt smiled slightly. "I'm glad that nickname is catching on."

It was the first time I laughed in weeks. The sensation felt good in my chest. It felt good everywhere.

"And it's okay. I should have been more understanding."

I shook my head in response.

"I forgive you, baby. I want to work this out—if you'll have me."

If I'll have him? Was he insane? "Of course I'll have you." I moved into his chest and hugged him tightly, welcoming his scent as it washed over me. His shirt smelled like mint and winter. His body was warm like a personal heater, and it welcomed me like I belonged.

Volt rested his chin on my head and ran his fingers through my hair. "I'm sorry I took so long."

"It's okay."

"I'm here now." He pressed his lips to my forehead and gave me a deep kiss. "And I'm not going anywhere."

***

Volt made dinner for me then served me on the couch.

"I'm not hungry."

"Baby, eat." He sat beside me and handed over the plate. It was a grilled cheese sandwich and tomato soup, just like the kind he made for Clay over Christmas break. "I can tell you haven't been eating enough." He eyed my arms, which were dangerously skinny.

I took a few bites of my soup and ate slowly, not used to the action of chewing.

Volt sat beside me, watching every move I made. "When you get your strength back, we can get to the good stuff." He winked then gave my thigh a gentle squeeze.

I ate faster, trying to down everything as quickly as possible.

Volt chuckled. "You missed me as much as I missed you."

I set the empty plate on the coffee table and immediately moved into his arms. I didn't care about sex, but I did want to cuddle. I wanted to be held forever and never be released. I wanted to sleep on his chest just the way I used to, to feel that comfort I once took for granted.

He lay back on the couch and pulled the blanket over both of us. His hand moved into my hair and he watched me with concerned eyes.

I was so happy to feel him underneath me I couldn't breathe. "I'm so glad you came. I didn't think you would."

"I'm sorry I took so long."

He had every right to be mad. I didn't hold it against him. "I'm surprised you changed your mind. You were really upset."

His fingers stopped in my hair. "Well, Sara paid me a visit."

I flinched at the sound of her name. "What did she want?"

"She asked me to forgive you. She said you really loved me and deserved another chance."

She did that? I couldn't believe what I was hearing.

Volt heard my unspoken thoughts. "I was surprised too. She said you were a mess without me. And she said we should be together since we love each other. Nothing else matters."

"And why did she do this?"

He shrugged. "I think she wanted to make things right for you."

"Because her plan backfired?" I hissed.

"I think she wants me to put in a good word for her to you. But I'm not sure if I can."

"How can asking you to take me back make up for what she did?" I asked coldly. "If she got her way, she never would have told us the truth."

"No. Probably not."

"Like I would ever forgive her."

Volt fell silent, stroking my hair once more. "I have some other news. Not sure how you're going to handle it."

If he slept with someone else, I didn't want to know about it. I just wanted to forget the whole thing and pretend it never happened. We could pick up where we left off and move on. "What?"

"I adopted Clay."

I heard what he said, but I couldn't process it. I sat up and looked down at him, needing to see the confirmation in his eyes. When I saw it, I gasped. "You're serious?"

He nodded, a slight smile on his lips. "About a week ago."

"What made you do that?"

He shrugged. "He's my family. He should live with me."

It was an incredibly sweet thing to do. I admired him more for it. "You think you can handle it?"

"I've been doing okay so far," he said. "And besides, I'll have help." His hand moved up my back, and he brought me closer to him. "I have a sexy teacher who can give me some pointers about teenagers."

If he told me this beforehand, I probably would have warned him about the responsibility. Being the guardian of a child was much different than tutoring him for an hour a day. But since everything had already been said and done, there was nothing left to do but be supportive. "I'm sure you don't need my help."

"I don't agree with that. Clay never had a mom around. He needs a mother figure in his life."

"And you think I'm the best candidate for the job?"

"Yep." He pulled me closer to his chest. "You're the only candidate for the job."

"Well, I'd be honored."

"And maybe we'll make a few of our own." He waggled his eyebrows at me.

"That sounds like fun." I tried to treasure this moment as much as possible. Last night, I slept alone in my bed and tried not to cry. Now, I had my life back. I had Volt back. Somehow, it was sweeter than it ever was before. Somehow, it was more beautiful. I appreciated it more when I didn't have it. And now that I did, I would never let go. "You want to practice now?"

His eyes lightened in excitement. "My moves have been getting rusty. We should probably test everything out."

Was that his way of telling me he didn't sleep with anyone else? Because if he didn't, it would just make things a million times better. But if he did, I didn't want to know about it. I didn't want to hear a single word about it.

Volt read the hesitation in my eyes. "Only you."

"Yeah?" My breath escaped my chest as a heave. I'd been holding my breath with dread, unprepared to hear the answer to a question I never asked.

"Yeah. I met this woman in a bar, and she wanted to hook up but...I didn't want to. So I just went home. I was so mad I thought I could do it. But my body still belonged to you—even if my mind was too pissed to understand that."

Music to my ears.

He saw the relief in my eyes. "I'm stuck on you, Taylor. You never have to worry about me looking for something else. Because I'm so hopelessly obsessed with you. I've been obsessed with you since the first time I looked at you. And I think I've been in love with you even longer."

Chapter Twenty-One

Volt

Taylor and I walked into the apartment, her bag of stuff over my shoulder. "Clay, I'm home." The TV was on in the living room, and I distinctly heard the sound of cars racing. He must be playing a video game.

"Hey."

"It's almost ten, Clay. You should be in bed." I held Taylor's hand as we walked into the living room.

His back was to us as he sat on the couch. "Fine. Whatever." He hit a few buttons on the controller and turned it off. "I was hoping you would be home later." He rose from the couch and walked around to greet me. "Oh, wow." He looked at Taylor with wide eyes. "You're back."

"I am." Taylor squeezed my hand.

"I took your advice, kid. I went out and got my girl," I said.

"Good," Clay said. "I was sick of you moping around all the time." He walked up to Taylor and gave her a hug. It was long and lingered for several seconds before he finally pulled away. "I'm glad you're back. It wasn't the same without you."

"Aww," Taylor whispered. "I'm happy to be back—with both of you."

"She's going to be staying with us for a while," I said. "Are you okay with that?" I was the adult and could do whatever I wanted, but this was Clay's home too. I wanted him to feel comfortable.

"Yeah, of course," he said. "I'm glad my room is on the other side of the apartment." He laughed then walked back into the sitting area. He put away his controller and cleaned up his area, returning it to how it looked before he used it.

"Wow," Taylor whispered. "You trained him well."

"Actually, I didn't do anything." He just did it on his own.

"Well, I'm going to get ready for bed." Taylor took the bag off my shoulder. "I'll see you soon."

"Okay."

She gave me a kiss before she walked down the hall.

I watched her go, grateful she wasn't a ghost from a memory.

When the bedroom door shut, I turned to Clay. "Thanks for the advice."

He shrugged. "I'm wise beyond my years. What can I say?"

I chuckled. "Yeah, I guess you are."

He put his hands in the pockets of his sweatpants. All his clothes were new, and I couldn't get over how different he looked. A new wardrobe, a shower, and a haircut made him a new person.

"How would you feel about her living here?"

"Like, forever?"

I nodded. "Would you be more comfortable if it's just us for a while?"

"Volt, it's your apartment. Do what you want."

"It's *our* apartment, Clay. You get a say in everything now."

His eyes softened even though he tried to hide it.

"What do you think?"

"I like Taylor. I don't mind having her around."

"You're sure about that?" I asked. "Because I'm going to ask her to move in. If you aren't ready, that's totally fine."

"No, I want her here."

"Yeah?"

He nodded.

"Okay. Then I'm going to ask her."

"I think it's a good idea. She cooks, right?"

I rolled my eyes. "Is that why you want her to move in? Because I cook for you."

"But I can't eat grilled cheese every day. I'll never poop."

Now I actually laughed. "Yeah, she's definitely a better cook."

"Then have her move in tomorrow."

"Alright. I'll ask."

He nodded then walked away. "I'm happy for you, Volt. You deserve it."

My heart ached when he said that. "Thanks..."

"I'll see you in the morning." He nodded to me then walked into his bedroom.

I listened to his door shut before I went back into the bedroom where Taylor waited for me. She was already dressed in one of my t-shirts with just her panties underneath. She was thinner than before, but just as sexy.

"Everything okay?" she asked.

"Yeah." I stripped down to my boxers and crawled into bed beside her. Our legs wrapped around each other, and our arms latched on to anything we could hold. We were tangled together, glued. Now that I had her, I intended to make love to her every night. I intended to cherish her and never let go. I intended to live happily ever after. "I asked him if it would be okay if you moved in with us."

She flinched in my arms, surprised and excited. "And what did he say?"

"He said he loved the idea. Then he asked if you cook."

She chuckled. "I know my way around the kitchen."

"I think we both need you—but for very different reasons."

She stared at me, her face pressed close to mine. She waited for me to ask her in words, to make it official.

"Baby, will you move in with me?"

Instead of smiling like I expected, her eyes watered. A loud sniff escaped her throat and she turned to mush beside me. Unable to answer, she just nodded.

Without realizing it, I felt my eyes water too. I felt guilty for putting her through hell. And I felt like shit for going through hell myself. "It's us from now on. It's you and me."

She nodded, her eyes still full of tears. "You and me."

***

Clay lifted a box from the floor and groaned. "Holy shit. What's in here?"

"Clay," I snapped.

"I mean, holy guacamole. What's in here?" He rolled his eyes at being berated for cussing.

Taylor chuckled. "Shoes. It says it right on the side of the box."

Clay shifted the box against his chest, using his core to support it. "Where does it go?"

"Put it in the office," Taylor said.

"What?" I asked. "Your shoes are going in my office?"

"Well, they're going in your closet," she said.

My man cave was slowly turning into a women's clothing store.

"Or I can put them in our room," she said. "But I'll have to make room."

And then my stuff would be shoved under the bed or something. "Yeah, put them in the office."

"Alright." Clay carried the box down the hall.

"Baby, you have so much shit."

"Shh!" She placed her forefinger over her lips. "Clay will hear you cuss."

"I heard that!" Clay shouted down the hall.

"Dammit," I whispered.

"I heard that too," Clay snapped.

I rolled my eyes. "That kid can hear crickets at night."

Taylor laughed then grabbed the next box in the pile. She examined the sides for a label, unsure what was inside.

I remained quiet and watched her.

"What's in here?" She lifted the box and realized it was light.

"I don't know," I said with a shrug. "You packed it."

"I labeled all my stuff. So I didn't pack it."

"Well, don't look at me," I said. "I didn't bring that in here."

She ripped open the lid and tore through the tape. She had to use her muscles to tear it open because it was compacted so tightly. When she finally broke through, she stared at the Styrofoam inside. "Maybe it's just extra packaging material."

I watched her.

She stuck her hand inside and felt around until she grabbed something. "No. There is something in here. What the hell is it? Maybe I packed it a long time ago and just forgot." She pulled out the small black box, the exact box I'd given to her once before.

She held it in her hand and fell silent as she looked at it. Her hand shook silently before she supported the box with her other palm. She stared at it in shock, unable to process exactly what was happening.

She looked at me with realization on her face. Her eyes knew exactly what it was. She knew exactly what was happening. Her eyes watered right on cue as the moment hit her.

I kneeled beside her and took the box from her hand. They were still shaking with tremors.

"Oh my god..." She covered her mouth. "Oh my fucking god."

I positioned the box and flipped the lid open, showing her the diamond ring I bought for her months ago. It was perfect for her, plain and simple but classy. My hand didn't shake as I held it out to her. The moment felt right. In fact, it felt out of place. I should have done this a long time ago. "Taylor Thomas, will you marry me?"

"Ahh!" She screamed into her hands, her face changing with a flood of emotions.

Without waiting for her to say yes, I pulled the ring out and grabbed her left hand.

"Yes." She sobbed as I placed the ring on her finger. "Yes. I'll marry you. Of course, I'll marry you."

It fit perfectly on her ring finger, nice and snug. The diamond sparkled in the light, showing a prism of color. Every time she moved, it dazzled. It looked perfect on her. It would look perfect on her for the rest of her life.

She extended her hand and stared at it. "Oh my god, it's beautiful. I love it." Her eyes lit up like glinting treasure and the light that radiated there couldn't be blocked out by any shadow. It was pure happiness, the same feeling that echoed deep in my heart.

"I'm glad."

She finally turned her gaze on me, so consumed with her ring I took a backseat. "I can't believe this..."

It was the perfect plan. Since I told her how I was going to propose when we broke up, I knew she wouldn't expect me to do it. But I wanted to do it like that anyway. Nothing else was more perfect.

"I love you." She wrapped her arms around my neck and kissed me.

"I love you too, baby."

She hugged me tightly, squeezing me with her limited strength. She started to cry again, sobbing into my chest. "I can't wait to spend my life with you, Muriel Rosenthal."

Despite the seriousness of the moment, I laughed. "Let's stick with Volt."

"Whatever you want, fiancé."

I kissed her forehead and felt her shake against me. This was the beginning of a happy life together. I would never forget what she said to me when we first met. She saw right through my playboy act, saw that I was hurting deep down inside. "You've made me so happy that I've forgotten what it was like to feel anything less."

She pulled away and looked into my eyes, recognizing her own words.

"And that's how I knew you were the one."

A new wave of tears emerged.

I never knew crying could be so beautiful. I always thought it was just annoying. But when she did it, it meant so much. When she cried in joy, it made me happy.

Clay stood there with my phone in his hand. He recorded the whole thing without her knowing about it. "Wait, hold on. Your real name is Muriel?"

My look of joy turned to one of irritation. I directed it on Taylor.

A guilty grin stretched across her face. "Whoops."

Epilogue

Volt

A crowd of five thousand people sat in the lines of chairs that faced the platform in front of the university. Students walked by, flipped their tassel, and then received their degree from the president of the university.

"Clay Rosenthal."

We jumped to our feet from the front row and clapped. Dad put his fingers in his mouth and whistled loudly. Mom dabbed her eyes with a handkerchief. "My grandson…"

Taylor clapped harder than anyone. "Go Clay!" Her parents stood beside her, cheering him on just as hard as she did.

Clay shook hands with the president and received his diploma. Then he pulled his tassel over, officially becoming a graduate. He found me in the office and waved, a smile on his face.

And then it hit me.

I wasn't an emotional guy.

But I got mushy.

My eyes sprang with tears because I was so immensely proud. He started off at the bottom and excelled to the top. Now he was walking across the stage with an honors chord around his neck.

Keep it together, man.

He walked off the stage and joined the other graduates.

We sat down and watched the other students receive their diplomas, but I wasn't paying attention to any of them. I was thinking about the day Clay left for college and how hard it was for me. I waited until he left to allow the tears to fall. And now here I was again, getting choked up.

"Aww…" Taylor caught the moisture in my eyes. "So proud."

"The sun is hurting my eyes."

"Whatever you say, babe." She patted my thigh.

***

After the ceremony was over, we located Clay in the chaotic crowd. He was standing near the pond, at the outreaches of the university so we could track him down.

When I spotted him, I felt the emotion creep up all over again. But I kept the reaction back, not wanting to act like my own parents. "Hey, graduate."

Clay walked over, as tall as me. He filled out as an adult, his arms bulging with muscle and his shoulders wide. When people saw us together, they thought we were brothers. "I did it. I finally graduated."

Finally? It seemed to pass in a blur.

I gripped both of his shoulders and looked him in the eye. "I can't tell you how proud I am."

Clay searched my expression, and the same look came into his eyes. He was vulnerable, everything pouring out. "I couldn't have done it without you."

"Yes, you could've. But I'm glad I made it easier for you." I squeezed his shoulders, feeling my heart ache with the love I had for this kid. He was my family. He may not be of my blood, but he was as good as.

"I wouldn't be here with you."

I pulled him in for a hug and felt my chest cave with emotion. "I love you so much…"

He squeezed me harder. "I love you too, Dad."

He never called me that before. I wasn't even sure if I heard it right. I pulled away, searching his expression for confirmation.

"You're my dad," he answered. "Can I call you that?"

Now I couldn't stop my eyes from watering. I couldn't stop the emotion that choked me from deep inside. And I wasn't even ashamed. "Of course. If that's what you want."

"It is."

I hugged him again, feeling like the proudest man in the world. He was a full-grown adult, but I hugged him like a child. I never knew him in his youth, but I felt like I'd known him his whole life. I was too young to feel this type of parental love. But I felt it nonetheless.

"Stop hogging him," Mom said. "We want a picture with our grandson."

I blinked my eyes quickly and pulled away. "You're right. He's all yours."

Taylor moved in next. Her pregnant belly was so big she was uncomfortable. I brought an umbrella for her so she could be in the shade at all times. Despite her enormous belly, she looked as beautiful as ever. In fact, she looked even more beautiful. "So proud of you, Clay." She had to turn her body so her belly wouldn't smash into him.

"Thanks."

"Your baby brother is proud of you too." She placed her hand on her stomach.

He did the same. "I'm sure he is. I can feel him kicking."

She kissed his cheek and gave him another squeeze. "Love you."

"Love you too, Mom."

Her eyes watered when he called her that. It was the first time she ever heard it. "We're both so happy for you, Son." She patted his shoulder before she stepped away, her hand immediately moving under her belly because it was more comfortable for her.

My attention turned to her now that Clay's grandparents moved in for pictures. "Baby, you need to sit down. There's a park bench right over there. How about some water?"

"I'm okay, Volt." Her eyes were on Clay. "I wouldn't miss this for anything."

I wrapped my arm around her waist. "Yeah...we did a good job."

"No, you did a good job. You saved his life, Volt."

"No." I didn't believe that. "He was the one who walked into my office in the first place. He wanted a better life for himself. He showed initiative."

"But he walked away. And you hunted him down. Don't downplay your role in this."

"I admit I helped. But he did all the work."

"You paid his tuition. Don't forget that."

I shrugged. "A smart kid would have made it happen anyway."

She smiled, clearly smitten by my humbleness. "I'm glad he'll be working in the city. We'll be able to see him all the time."

"I know." Now I understood how my parents felt when I moved back after college. They were thrilled to the point of tears. I pulled her closer against me, feeling so grateful that my life turned out so well. I had the woman of my dreams on my arm, and I had another son on the way. Could life get any better?

"Can you take a picture of me and my dad?" Clay asked.

I would never get tired of hearing him call me that. It fit so well. I walked away from Taylor and went to his side.

Clay handed me his diploma. "You hold it."

"Why?"

"Because this is all happening because of you."

Everyone awed quietly as they watched us.

I took it from his hand and held it up.

Clay put his arm around me and smiled for the camera.

I smiled too but felt a lot more than joy. I felt a million things at once. I never knew I could love someone the way I loved Clay. I never knew someone could change my life so much—in the best way possible. He claimed I saved him, but he saved me too. He made me into a better man, made me into a guy worthy of Taylor. He prepared me for fatherhood, for my next son about to be born. He gave me so much without realizing it.

When the picture was taken, Clay waved Taylor over. "Can I get a picture with both of them?"

Mom held up the camera. "Of course. It's your day."

Taylor walked to his other side. "I'm going to look like a cow in these pictures."

"A hot cow, maybe," I said.

"Mom, you look beautiful." He wrapped his arm around her waist.

She melted for him in a way she never melted for me. Her eyes locked to mine and an unspoken conversation happened between us. She had as much of a role in his life as I did, and together, we made a great team. We made a difference in the classroom, in the tutoring program, and with a boy who just needed help.

I thought Sara was the one, but she was just a placeholder until the right woman came along. Taylor was my other half, the woman I was destined to spend my life with. She was the only woman who could ever fix me, who could put my life back together. She stuck beside me through the hard times, and we made it to the other side. There was no doubt she and I were supposed to be together, to live happily ever after.

Now I couldn't remember a time when I miserable. I'd been happy for so long I couldn't imagine a different way of life. It seemed like it'd always been this way. I'd always been happy.

And I would always be happy.

Dear Reader,

Thank you for reading Combust. I hope you enjoyed reading it as much as I enjoyed writing it. If you could leave a short review, it would help me so much! Those reviews are the best kind of support you can give an author. Thank you!

Wishing you love,

E. L. Todd

Want to check out my next series?

Ray of Light is a fun romance, guaranteed to make you laugh and cry.

Available Now

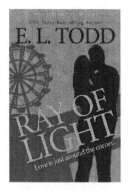

My brother is an idiot. He won the lottery and invested all of his money in a run-down bowling alley. Since he's barely making it, he moved in with me.

Great.

Having him around the house isn't the worst thing in the world, but he does make a mess like nobody's business. My friends Zeke, Jessie, and Kayden keep me sane but there's only so much they can do.

And it's definitely not the worst thing in the world when his old friend, Ryker, moves to town.

The second I lay eyes on him, I'm hot under the collar. He makes my body burn in longing and freeze in desperation at the exact same time. When he talks, I don't listen to anything he says because I'm staring at that hard jaw and those kissable lips like I already own them.

But he's a bed hopper. A playboy. A heartbreaker.

I'm all down for some hot, sweaty, yummy sex even if it doesn't have a fairy tale ending. I've been down that road before. I know the drill. But with Ryker, it's different.

Because I know I'll fall in love with him.

For now, I'll steer clear of him and keep my hands to myself. It can't be that hard, right?

Or can it?

Want To Stalk Me?

Subscribe to my newsletter for updates on new releases, giveaways, and for my comical monthly newsletter. You'll get all the dirt you need to know. Sign up today.

www.eltoddbooks.com

Facebook:

https://www.facebook.com/ELTodd42

Twitter:

@E_L_Todd

Now you have no reason not to stalk me. You better get on that.

EL's Elites

I know I'm lucky enough to have super fans, you know, the kind that would dive off a cliff for you. They have my back through and through. They love my books, and they love spreading the word. Their biggest goal is to see me on the New York Times bestsellers list, and they'll stop at nothing to make it happen. While it's a lot of work, it's also a lot of fun. What better way to make friendships than to connect with people who love the same thing you do?

Are you one of these super fans?

If so, send a request to join the Facebook group. It's closed, so you'll have a hard time finding it without the link. Here it is:

https://www.facebook.com/groups/1192326920784373

Hope to see you there, ELITE!

Made in the USA
Lexington, KY
07 April 2017